D1473900

Trail of the Circle Star

Other Avalon Books by Lee Martin

TRAIL OF THE HUNTER
TRAIL OF THE LONG RIDERS
TRAIL OF THE FAST GUN
DEAD MAN'S WALK

TRAIL OF THE CIRCLE STAR

****

LEE MARTIN

AVALON BOOKS
THOMAS BOUREGY AND COMPANY, INC.
401 LAFAYETTE STREET
NEW YORK, NEW YORK 10003

PRINTED IN THE UNITED STATES OF AMERICA
ON ACID-FREE PAPER
BY HADDON CRAFTSMEN, SCRANTON, PENNSYLVANIA

To James Liontas, founder of Peninsula University Law School, my alma mater. Jim is a modern-day hero fighting for justice and equality. He would have been a judge or worn a badge in the Old West.

Chapter One

*D*eputy U.S. Marshal Hank Darringer was riding toward the distant, violent town of Prospect, Colorado, on a spring morning in 1878. He followed the north bank of the busy Rocky River, riding among the cottonwoods. He was excited, eager to see his cousin, the man he idolized.

But he suddenly reined to a halt. With the loud noise of the river to his left, he sat straight in the saddle, gazing at the hanged man dangling from a tree just ahead.

Looking grim, with his square jaw set and perspiration on his slightly hooked nose, Hank was afraid to ride forward. Tossing its head, his black stallion, muscles rippling, became restless.

Hank Darringer swallowed hard. There was something familiar about the big man hanging from the crooked limb of the cottonwood. Like Hank, the man wore a black leather vest over a blue shirt, was broad shouldered and lean, and had collar-length, dark-brown hair.

Though the dead man's back was to him, Hank

was sweating heavily and his mouth was dry as bone. He could feel his heart drumming in his chest. Breath tight, he allowed his stallion to walk slowly forward.

The earth was caked mud, cut with prints Hank figured were a day old. He rode forward, reining up when he saw the circled star on the man's vest.

Hank felt sick to his stomach as he gazed at the face of his cousin, Marshal Bob Harrington. Hank's mentor and good friend, the man who had taught him the meaning of the badges they both wore, had been murdered.

Tears in his dark-gray eyes, Hank dismounted, drew his hunting knife from his belt, and cut the rope secured to the trunk of the tree. He sheathed the blade and turned quickly to catch the falling body and lower it to the ground. "Easy there, Bob," he muttered huskily. "I've got you now."

His voice sounded strange. Ignoring the tears running down his hot face, Hank discovered with anger that the lawman had been shot in the back and—judging by his distorted face—his cousin had been alive when hanged.

A violent desire for vengeance flared up in Hank. As he removed the rope, he couldn't help remembering what his cousin had said just a few months ago: "Hank, there ain't nothin' you can do about right or wrong. What you gotta do is track 'em down and haul 'em in. No more, no less."

Bob Harrington's counsel had made sense, until now. Bitter anger rose within Hank as he tied the dead man across his saddle. Then he removed his possibles long enough to get a blanket from the bedroll behind his saddle. He covered his cousin's body as well as he could.

Unable to move, he stood a moment, his face hot and wet with tears. Looking down at the circled star on his own vest, he remembered last fall when Bob had pinned it on for him in Denver and Marshal Wilcox had sworn him in.

Hank had worn a town marshal's badge in the Dakotas, but nothing had hit him like the honor of wearing this star, especially since he had just received a pardon for some old Texas trouble. His cousin's dedication and pride had inspired Hank. But now Hank was fighting mad.

Taking the reins of his restless black stallion, he turned and followed the river toward the distant town. Someone was going to pay for this. And right now, a badge would be more of a hindrance than a help in bringing the murderers to justice.

As he neared the town, he saw that saloons and gambling halls lined the road across from Rocky River. Perhaps he'd find his cousin's killers in one of them, he reflected grimly.

Seeing Hank coming, an old man on a mule had spun about to ride back up the street to the Silver Palace Saloon. There, Stumpy Potts jumped down from his mule and hobbled into the deserted establishment. Squinting in the poor light, the little white-haired man called out in a frantic, raspy voice, "Anybody here?"

From the back office, Silas Tanner emerged, wearing his brocade smoking jacket. Tall and slim, with a thin black mustache and swarthy skin, Tanner was a handsome man in his forties. He grimaced with distaste when he saw the little informer, but the old man asked for little more than drinks and meals in exchange for what was sometimes useful information.

"Stumpy, I gave you money last night," Tanner reminded him.

"We're in a lot of trouble," the little man announced. "There's a U.S. Deputy Marshal comin' this way."

"So?"

"He's been at the hangin' tree. And he's Hank Darringer."

"I heard of the Darringers," Silas said, unimpressed. "Just a bunch of gunfighters."

"I seen this here fella up in Dakota once. He took four fellas in a facedown gunfight. Got all of 'em, and he wasn't even scratched."

"So?"

"Fastest draw I ever seen. And he didn't bat an eye."

"Stumpy, you're worried for nothin'."

"I figure this here deputy ain't gonna ride on till he finds out who hanged Marshal Harrington. And when he starts pokin' around, he's gonna find out a lot of other things, ain't he?"

"Whatever he finds we'll blame on the vigilantes. But just in case, you tell the Smith boys I want to see them."

Stumpy turned, hobbled back to the door, and peered out. "Here he comes."

From the darkness of the saloon, they squinted into the bright sunlight. A tall, lean man with wide shoulders was silhouetted against the morning sun. His black, wide-brimmed hat was pulled down tight on his brow, and he wore a black leather vest with a shining star. He was leading a powerful black stallion, a dead man tied across the saddle.

As he neared, the men in the saloon drew back, remaining out of sight. But Tanner foresaw plenty of trouble as he gazed at the lawman's face. About thirty, the man wore a .45 Army Colt in a cut-down holster hung at his right hip and strapped to his thigh. The butt of a Winchester repeater jutted from his scabbard.

Hank Darringer knew he was being watched and could be going to his death. Whoever had shot and hanged his cousin wasn't fond of lawmen. Yet he was so angry, he would welcome any action that invited retaliation.

He glanced to his left at the hurried Rocky River, a twenty-feet-wide stretch of sparkling white water heading east toward green cattle country and the distant prairie. Its banks were dotted with cottonwoods and scrub oak. The river came raging out of the Rocky Mountains, which rose behind the foothills in great, snow-crested peaks against the western sky.

Prospect was set in wooded hills, great land for cattle, with plenty of lush new grass and water. Oaks, aspens, cottonwoods, junipers, and service-berry thickets were also plentiful, as well as bob-cats, red foxes, mule deer, coyotes, and rattle-snakes. The slopes were home for black bears and mountain lions.

Higher in the ridges, silver and gold were being mined. Greed was rampant, and vigilantes were out of control.

"I don't care how you do it," Wilcox had told Bob. "Just clean up that rat hole. Hank can join you as soon as he delivers a prisoner to Canon City."

By the time he neared the Silver Palace Saloon, Hank had already passed a gambling hall, four sa-loons, a dance hall, and the Miners' Hotel, all lined up north of the river.

Now the muddy road turned abruptly to the right. As he turned his back on the river, to his left was the huge, grand Hotel Prospect. Up above it in the green hills were a small white church and a red schoolhouse. Farther up and to the north was a white mansion with ornate gables.

He tied his horse at the railing in front of the sheriff's office, a frame building with no front win-dows. Across the street were Hattie's Eatery, vari-ous stores, the bank, and the newspaper office.

Other buildings housed the local barber, doctor,

post office, stage depot, express office, gunsmith, blacksmith, and livery.

The street was empty except for a few horses and wagons and a string of twenty pack mules loaded with iron rails to be dragged to the mines. The town was still asleep.

His burning face grim, Hank drew his Winchester from its scabbard, resting his hand for just a moment on the body beneath the blanket. Then he walked onto the boardwalk and shoved open the door to the sheriff's office.

Maybe fifty, the local sheriff wore a star on his dirty shirt. He was stretched out on a bunk and snoring. The front of the jail had rifle slots. On each side was a tall window with wooden shutters. Three empty cells in back had tiny, high windows.

Near the desk sat a cold stove. Faded Wanted posters, seemingly old and forgotten, covered the wall behind the big heavy chair.

Hank used his rifle barrel to poke the stout man on the bunk. Startled by the rifle in his side, the sheriff opened his pale brown eyes, his wide mouth gaping under a heavy brown mustache.

Hank drew back, his badge gleaming in the light from the open door. The sheriff blinked.

"I take it you're Sheriff Smite," Hank observed dryly.

"Yeah, sure, but who the devil are you?"

"Deputy U.S. Marshal Hank Darringer."

Feeling mighty perturbed, Smite stood up, and was annoyed to find that Hank was even taller. He had heard that the Darringers were nothing but gunfighters. Quickly lighting a fire in the stove, he set a cold pot of old coffee on top of it. Then he went behind the desk, looking self-important as he sat in the big chair. "So, what are you doing here?" he demanded.

"I came to meet with Marshal Harrington."

Smite grimaced. "That so?"

"He's out there on my saddle. I found him down in the cottonwoods. Someone shot him in the back, then hanged him."

"I don't know nothin' about that."

Hank studied the man for a long moment. "He was here to clean up this town."

"Nothin' wrong with Prospect. We don't need no outside law."

"He was also lookin' for some men who killed a U.S. Marshal and an express guard about three years ago over in Dodge City. One of 'em was named France, supposed to be about fifty with white hair. An anonymous letter went from Prospect to Denver, sayin' they were here. You got any ideas?"

Obviously uninterested, Smite leaned back in his chair, shaking his head.

"He didn't have the poster on him," Hank said. "You got another?"

"Nope. Never seen one like that."

"Where's the undertaker?" Hank asked, his anger rising.

"Well, the barber sorta does that for us. He's

next door. And if you want a preacher, he's up on the hill."

Since he could see there would be no help from this man, Hank grimly went outside and led his stallion up the street to the barber's.

Eyes burning, Hank delivered his cousin's body to the whiskered barber.

"Don't you worry none," the man said. "You come back in an hour. I'll get the preacher to read over 'im. But don't expect any mourners."

Hank went back outside. People were stirring, mostly headed for Hattie's Eatery. Some were curious, but others apparently were not surprised to see a dead man across a saddle. After carrying the body indoors, Hank mounted his big stallion and rode up the street.

Beyond the livery were the freight lines, and, across from them, the volunteer fire department. A common sight in foothill towns, riderless horses, rented to the miners, were trailing back from the northern mountain road, heading for home in the livery.

"I do a great business," the fat, grinning owner of the livery informed Hank as he put up his horse. "Them miners come down in the ore wagons over to the smelter, north of town by the sawmill. Once they have their hoot, they gotta get back home. And of course, I rent to newcomers who wanta get up there."

After leaving his gear in the stall, Hank carried

his saddlebags and his Winchester to the open doors facing the wide, dusty street.

"You can get a meal at Hattie's Eatery by the hotel," the fat man said. "Bear or venison, about two bits. But you go to the Prospect Hotel, you gotta pay five times that, just so you get a table-cloth."

"Thanks."

"Now the Prospect, that'll cost you about three dollars a night, but over to the Miners' Hotel, maybe a dollar, if you don't mind crowdin'."

Hank turned and walked along the boardwalk toward the hotel. The buildings were all faded from the winter. Most had glass windows and curtains. Lanterns hung in front of various buildings. Over-head, a black buzzard was sailing the wind in the clear blue sky.

Hank felt grimy and in need of a bath, but he walked slowly. His steel-gray eyes scanned the buildings on both sides. Word would get out fast that he was here.

Smite came out on the boardwalk. Hank joined him, thinking the man might have some word for him. Instead, the sheriff was just curious:

"So, how long you gonna be here?"

"Long enough."

Smite grimaced. "You'd better watch your step. There are some powerful men around here."

"Such as?"

"Well, there's Silas Tanner, who owns the Silver Palace and a few other establishments. And there's ol' Harris Sloan, a big cattle rancher. Then there's some plenty tough mine owners and freight operators. And Roan Carter. He owns the Prospect Mine and half the town. He's one feller you don't cross. And he's got somethin' else."

"And that is?"

"His daughter, Rosalee. Prettiest blamed female in the whole state of Colorado. No man can get near her, and it ain't accounta her Pa. She's plenty tough all by herself. Wait'll you see her ridin' side-saddle, all gussied up, with a Smith & Wesson in her purse."

"Sounds interestin'."

"Forget it, Darringer. Besides, men like you run out o' time mighty fast. Won't be long before you tangle with the likes of the Smith brothers."

"Gunmen?"

"There's three of 'em. Mean as sin. One's big as a barn, likes to break men with his hands. The other two are always spoilin' for a fight. They mostly work for Tanner."

"Nobody in this town is wanted."

Balancing his Winchester and his saddlebags over his shoulder, Hank turned away. The sheriff was trying to scare him out of town.

But Smite was right about one thing: Lawmen didn't live very long, especially if they stood for law and order and didn't take anything under the table. Bob had taught him that honesty and integrity were essential. Hank had always looked up to his cousin as a hero of sorts, the kind of man he wished he could be. Wearing a badge had become Hank's life.

The anger in him had not faded, though it had given way to feverish preparations. Somehow, he would find the killers—even if he had to tear this town apart.

He walked over to the Prospect Hotel, finding it grand in every way possible. The front porch was set with ornate white benches and large plants hanging in baskets. In the lobby were plush blue-upholstered furniture and a shining red-brown piano. The windows had lace-panel curtains and heavy blue drapes. Beyond the lobby was an equally plush dining room.

Hank took a room overlooking the street. Peering through the lace curtains, he looked down on the veranda. He could see the shining river in the distance. Across the street, the sheriff was hurrying toward the saloons.

It was Sunday morning. Hank expected there would soon be streams of people headed for the church on the hillside.

After bathing, shaving, and changing his clothes, Hank put his vest and gleaming badge back on. He went outside and down to the barber's.

Four merchants had volunteered to help at the burial. Up on the pretty hillside behind the church, the little white-haired preacher spoke all the right words in the small cemetery.

Hank stayed alone by the grave for some time.

His cousin had been buried with his star on his vest, a tribute to a good lawman.

Finally, Hank said good-bye to his cousin and went back to his room at the hotel. He felt choked, out of breath. Tears stung his eyes, but his grief was soon replaced by fury. He paced about, fighting for control.

Finally he forced himself to leave the hotel and walk to Hattie's Eatery, a big building with long tables. Twenty or so men were already seated and stuffing themselves. Hank sat apart from them, alone with his back to the wall. Some of the men looked as hard as nails.

The plump woman serving him was Hattie, he soon discovered. She had a good, round face and bright blue eyes, and she wore her brown hair in a bun. Her smile was wide and friendly as she wiped her hands on her white apron and said, "You look hungry, Marshal."

He proved her right, downing the scrambled eggs and bacon as if he had never eaten in his life. She brought him seconds and steaming hot coffee. He smiled up at her.

"Can you sit with me?" he asked.

"Since my feet hurt, I can sit a minute. What do you want to know?" Grinning, she plunked down across from him.

"Maybe I just want your company."

"Maybe birds don't fly."

"Maybe we'll be friends."

"I'd like that."

"But first—have you got any idea who killed Marshal Harrington?"

"Sure, about fifty of 'em. I got to warn you, Marshal. Nobody around here wants the law, except some of us business folks. Men get shot all the time. Hanged too."

"Are the vigilantes organized?"

"No. What you got is maybe a dozen men one time, and a whole new bunch another, just takin' the law in their own hands. The sheriff, he's smart enough to stick to his mendin'."

"And you don't see any particular motive in Harrington's bein' shot and hanged?"

"Well, he was wearin' a badge just like yours, and he was probably pokin' his nose around where it wasn't wanted. You gotta remember, Marshal, a lot of folks here, especially up at the mines, they ain't wearin' the same name they was born with."

"How about you, Hattie?"

"I ain't talkin'," she said, grinning. As he stood up, she sobered. "But I got to warn you. Them three Smith brothers been killin' right and left. Tanner sets 'em on anybody he don't like."

Hank thanked her and went outside, feeling content with a full belly. He looked toward the river road and wondered if the sheriff was still down in the saloons, passing the word about his presence in town.

Then he looked north and was stopped cold.

Two riders were approaching. One, a husky man of average height, sat on his bay as if he owned the town. He was wearing a store-bought suit and a fancy blue vest, and a pipe was stuck in his wide mouth. His face, with its short mustache, was hard as nails. A small-brimmed hat was set back on his gray-streaked brown hair.

Next to him, carrying a riding crop and riding sidesaddle on a black mare, was a woman of about twenty. Tall and slender in a fancy blue velvet riding outfit, she carried a riding crop. A velvet purse was slung about her waist, and her long black hair was flying loose and silken in the sunlight.

As she neared, he saw that face more clearly. She was the most beautiful woman he had ever seen. There was something wild about her, exotic, dangerous. Her eyes were dark, blue maybe. Her full lips and high cheekbones made her look proud. She sat the saddle as if she were a princess.

The pair reined up in front of the hotel. As they dismounted, Hank started slowly toward them. The woman was first on the boardwalk, pausing to look at him.

"Looks like we have us another lawman in town," the man said. "My name's Roan Carter, Marshal. This is my daughter, Rosalee."

A foot shorter than Hank, she stood as tall as she possibly could, head back, blue eyes glistening. After a long look at Hank, she allowed a smile on her pretty lips.

"Hank Darringer," he said, tipping his hat.

The rancher and his daughter were both surprised. The name of Darringer meant gunfighter, even with a badge.

"You go on inside, Rosalee," Carter said.

She turned and went up the stairs, her full skirts swishing about her. Soft and shiny, her ebony hair reached to her slim waist. Hank couldn't take his eyes from her.

"Now then, Marshal, to what do we owe this visit?"

"The murder of Marshal Harrington."

"I heard about that when I was ridin' in. Mighty sorry. I suggest you go up to the mines. There are some surly men up there."

"I might do that."

Hank nodded and turned to walk up the street, still shaken by the sight of Rosalee. Women had never been a part of his life. He had never had time for them. She was the first to get his attention. All of a sudden, he was thinking about settling down. The shock of that still vibrated.

"You there, Marshal."

Hank slowly turned and looked across the street toward the barber's, where three men stood lounging in the shade. Their very presence caused others to pause and watch.

One man was big and hairy, apelike. His face was half covered with black beard and mustache. His nose was flat from a prior fight, and he had huge arms and beady eyes. Next to him was a small, bug-eyed man with a crooked mouth. The third man was mean-eyed and had a skinny nose.

All three men wore cut-down holsters, a strong indication they were killers. Hank decided they had to be the Smith brothers, though obviously Smith wasn't their real name. There was a good possibility they had killed his cousin.

Evidently the leader, the small, bug-eyed man walked into the street, pushing his hat back from his dirty brow. "I hear you're one of them Darringers," he snarled. "Well, me and my brothers, we figure we don't need no Federal law around here. And I ain't one bit afraid of you. So why don't you just come on over?"

Hank was aware that the whole town was watching. He saw faces peering from windows as men cleared the street. A woman shoved her child quickly into the post office. Riders spun about for safety. The rush was followed by heavy silence.

"Come on, Marshal. I ain't gonna hurt you."

For a long moment Hank considered what to do. If he turned and walked away, the town would see it as weakness and he would become more of a target. If he drew on the man, the other brothers would make it three against one. Yet Hank had to do something.

He leaned on a post, shaking his head.

The bug-eyed Smith's mouth twitched with new anger. He took a few steps closer, his hands at his side. Still Hank didn't move. The man walked to the center of the dusty street. Then, furious that Hank hadn't moved, he walked even closer.

Now Hank slowly walked from the boardwalk

into the street. He was only ten feet from the man, but he kept walking toward him. Uneasy at Hank's steady pace, the gunman backed away slightly, resting his hand near his holster. Now Hank was only five feet away.

Suddenly the nervous man reached for his gun, and Hank sprang forward, slamming his fist into the man's face. He heard bones crack. Gun in hand, Smith staggered backward, his free hand clutching his face in horror. He raised his gun to fire.

Hank hit him again, this time in the middle. The man doubled up and gasped, sinking to his knees. Hank kicked the gun from his hand, then straightened.

The two brothers on the boardwalk looked grim and tense, but neither moved. Hank kicked the gun farther down the street, keeping his eye on them. Now he paused, waiting.

For a long moment, the brothers studied the situation. Then the apelike man slowly went into the street, retrieved the gun, and grabbed his fallen brother by the arm, half dragging him into the alley and over to the stairs to the doctor's office.

The third brother, the one with the mean eyes and skinny nose, was still standing there. His mouth twisted into a sneer as he snarled, "You're a dead man, Marshal."

Hank felt a cold chill run up and down his spine. He knew he could get shot in the back. Yet his anger at his cousin's death sustained him, and he stood steadfast as the man turned to follow his brothers.

Drawing a long breath, Hank walked over to the newspaper office. The door was open. A clean-shaven man with blond hair was busy setting type at a long counter facing the wall. He had ink all over his clothes and hands when he turned to smile at his visitor and said, "Stumpy Potts has already told me about you, Marshal. I'm Nelson F. Gibney, editor extraordinaire. I saw you with the Smiths. They work for Tanner. And you took a big chance."

"Maybe."

"I also saw you talking to Rosalee. I have to tell you that I plan to marry her, so you can just forget whatever you had in mind."

"If you were sure of yourself, you wouldn't have to be sayin' it."

"Let me explain something to you, Marshal. I'm an educated man. Rosalee's father finds that very important."

"And what about Rosalee?"

"She's a princess. And you'd be a poor prospect, Marshal. Besides, I understand that lawmen don't live very long out West."

"Like Bob Harrington."

"I can't tell you much about that," Gibney said. "No one knows anything."

Hank looked around the newspaper office. On one wall was a set of narrow drawers on which rested trays of type. A stove was in the corner.

Three tables were covered with newsprint. A hand-press stood near the left wall, type set in a tray, waiting for the cranks to turn.

"A little dirty," Gibney said apologetically.

"But somethin' to be proud of. Reckon I've seen a few editors run out of town, or shot, just for speakin' their mind."

"Are you asking why I'm still alive?"

"Maybe."

"I can manage to print news without editorializing."

"That the way you want it?"

Gibney winced, and Hank turned, walking back outside. He was sorry he had accused the editor of playing it safe. Every man had to find his own road.

He stood on the boardwalk and watched the townspeople moving up the green hillside toward the little white church. From the hotel, Rosalee and her father were also heading up the trail.

Hank moved toward them, deciding it was time to go to church. He thought of his three brothers and how their determined mother had dragged them all to church down in Texas. She was probably doing the same with the new brood she was bringing up with her second husband, another Darringer.

Turning, he saw men coming from the saloons to join the merchants and ladies. One man in particular stood out, a tall, slim, well-dressed man in a black coat. His stride conveyed arrogance and pride.

"That's Silas Tanner," Gibney told Hank. The editor had put on his coat, but his hands were still stained with ink. "He'd like to marry Rosalee."

"Is she the only single woman around here?"

"No, but the others can't be compared to her."

Hank started walking, Gibney at his side. Together, they soon turned up the hill toward the church. Gibney seemed amused. "You're wasting your time, Marshal," he said. "Your going to church won't impress Rosalee or her father. I've told you, education is everything. She's had some schooling in Philadelphia. And I went to Harvard."

Hank ignored him and led the way. At the church, they filed inside. The noisy congregation was still being seated. A woman was playing a small organ in the far corner. The preacher stood behind the plain wooden pulpit.

Rosalee and her father sat in a front pew. The aisle seat next to her was empty. Gibney tried to get there first, but Hank was too quick.

As he sat down beside her, Hank removed his hat and smoothed his collar-length brown hair. Startled, she turned to look at him, her dark blue eyes glistening with distrust.

"That seat is taken," she said.

"Just wanted to see if you smelled like roses. But it's lilacs," he said softly.

She blushed but smiled. Then Gibney came to stand at his side, waiting. Hank stood up, swept his hat over the seat, and gave it to the perturbed editor.

Satisfied, but wondering at his own nerve, Hank went to a back pew and sat next to a young woman in a blue gingham dress. He didn't notice her at first, but then he realized she was watching him.

"Marshal, I'm Melanie Sloan. My father's not here to introduce us properly," she told him shyly.

She was pretty, her blue eyes twinkling and her blond hair done up in large curls. There was something sweet and innocent about her smile. Her complexion was the color of peaches.

"Glad to meet you," he said awkwardly.

"I'm sure my father would like to have you to supper one night soon."

Hank nodded his acceptance, but his glance kept returning to the front pew and the long, silken black hair of a woman who was like no one he had ever met.

The church services began. The short, excited preacher delivered a sermon filled with fire and brimstone. His sometimes squeaky voice carried all the way to the heavens. He often waved his arms and pounded his fist.

During one of the hymns, Rosalee stood up by the organ and sang. Rising with the words, her voice was clear, sweet, and unbelievably beautiful. Her face was so wonderful, it hurt Hank to watch her. Maybe he was a fool to pursue the unobtainable. Yet Darringers didn't know how to backtrack.

"There are stories about her," Melanie whispered.

Hank shrugged, twisting the brim of his hat in his hand.

Abruptly, Hank stood up and walked outside into the bright sun. Even as he headed down the hillside, he could still hear Rosalee's sweet clear voice.

He was halfway down the slope when a rifle shot cracked the air. The bullet slammed into the front of his left shoulder, spinning him around as the shot echoed. He staggered back, his right hand drawing his Colt. Again the rifle barked, the bullet creasing his forehead but knocking him backward.

Stunned, he crashed back into the grass as another shot rang loud in the morning air.

Chapter Two

A s people rushed out of the church door, Hank lay sprawled and unconscious in the deep green grass. Some of the men ran to him, among them the short, balding doctor.

At the door, Melanie put her white-gloved hands to her face and looked away, retreating back inside the church. Silas Tanner stood outside in the sunlight and smoothed his mustache, his dark eyes gleaming. On the trail below, Sheriff Smite took his time walking up the hill.

Unable to calm his congregation, the preacher let them go. Rosalee and her father went outside with the crowd, then paused to watch as two men carried the Federal lawman down the slope. Smite and the doctor followed.

"Shouldn't someone be looking for the gunman?" Rosalee asked.

"Stay out of it," her father muttered.

"It's just terrible," Melanie said to them. "I won't sleep tonight."

Rosalee nodded politely. Her father stuck his

pipe in his mouth and took her arm. They walked down to the boardwalk near the hotel. "Let's go home," he said.

Rosalee hesitated as Nelson Gibney joined them. "Are you all right?" he asked her.

She smiled at his concern. "Yes."

"I'm going up to see what the story is," Gibney told them.

"You're in more of a hurry than usual," Carter grunted.

"Well, just this morning, someone reminded me what my job was. Miss Rosalee, may I still call on you tomorrow afternoon?"

She nodded. "Of course."

Gibney took her hand and bowed slightly. Then he turned away, crossing the street toward the doctor's office.

Carter helped his daughter mount her black mare. She settled onto the sidesaddle, waiting as he mounted. Then the two of them rode north up the street. Many people paused to look at the lovely brunette and her father.

Once they were out of town, Carter turned to her and said, "Maybe it's time you said yes to Gibney."

"Please don't rush me, Father."

"He's well educated. He knows how to earn his living. He'd take good care of you if somethin' was to happen to me."

"Father, nothing will happen to you."

"I want you taken care of, Rosalee. I don't want anyone ever lookin' down at you. I want 'em always to be lookin' up. And any of 'em that whisper, I'll blow their heads off."

"But don't you think I should at least be honest with Gibney?"

"What, and tell him your ma was one-quarter Cheyenne? Just how do you think he'd react? He's from a fine family in Pennsylvania. How do you think they'd feel about it? And what about the people here, some of 'em havin' lost folks in Indian fights?"

"Well, I lost my grandmother at Sand Creek."

"I never shoulda told you that," he growled. "And that was fourteen years ago. Chivington was a fool to run that massacre against Black Kettle. It caused the Cheyenne to sack and burn Julesburg, and got Denver isolated for years. But that's all history, Rosalee."

"But it's part of my history."

"No, it's not. You're only one-eighth Cheyenne, and that ain't enough to tell anyone about."

"I'm proud of my heritage. I'm not afraid."

"You do as I say and marry Gibney. If he finds out, he'll be too much of a gentleman to do anything. That's why he's the one for you."

"I still hate this secrecy."

"You'll have to trust me, Rosalee. I know what's best. Now, you be extra nice to Gibney tomorrow."

Distressed by the conversation, she rode on in silence. But she kept seeing the hard, handsome face of the new lawman. She sensed the town would never be the same again.

* * *

The afternoon dragged on as the doctor removed
bullets from the unconscious lawman. When Hank
finally awakened late that night, he was alone in
a darkened room. He could hear voices in the next
room. Gibney was apparently questioning the doctor, who sounded irritated: "Listen here, Gibney,
I got better things to do than talk with you."

"But, Doc, whoever shot this man most likely
killed Harrington. I have to wait until he's conscious. It's a story for my paper. Why, it could have
been the Smiths."

"I have men up here with bullet holes every day
of the week. I don't believe folks out there are particular who they hit. Now, will you get out of here
and let me get some sleep? It's near midnight."

"Can I see if he's awake?"

"You're loco, you know that, Gibney? Sure, go
ahead."

The door opened and light struck Hank Darringer. He was lying on a bunk against the wall.
Bandages prevented his sore left shoulder and arm
from moving. His throbbing head was also bandaged. He squinted in the light.

"Doc, he's awake."

The medical man was short, bald, and grumpy.
He came in and turned up a lamp to check Hank's
vision and condition.

"Your head's made of iron," the doctor said.
"But you'd better sleep here tonight."

Hank forced himself to sit up. "Not likely." Despite the doctor's protests, he got to his feet, checked his holster to be sure he was armed, and pulled his hat on his bandaged head. Dizzy, he put a hand on Gibney's shoulder. The editor took him out of the office, onto a porch, and down a flight of stairs to the boardwalk.

They paused in front of the barber's so Hank could steady himself. It was dark except for street lanterns and an occasional lighted window. The moonless night was cold.

Gibney helped him across the dusty street.

"You started out with a bang," the editor commented.

"I reckon no one saw where it came from."

"No, but they got you in the left shoulder, and the angle indicates the shot could have come anywhere from my place north along the street."

"They didn't waste any time."

"Melanie was sure upset."

"You trying to get my mind off Rosalee?"

"Why not? I already told you she was taken."

"She promised to you?"

"No, but listen, Marshal, she's not for you."

"Because of the stories?"

"You heard those too? Well, it's nonsense. She has some Spanish blood, that's all. And it's Spanish aristocracy, besides. She doesn't have a drop of Indian blood."

Hank was surprised but pretended he had already heard the rumor. "But what if the stories were true?"

"But they're not," Gibney said, sidestepping the issue.

"If they were, would you marry her?"

"Blast you, Darringer. I didn't ask you to be my conscience."

They entered the hotel, Hank now able to move on his own. He said good night to the editor and made his way up the stairs, reaching his room exhausted and still in pain.

He lay on his bed and stared at the ceiling in the pale light of the lamp. Rosalee was so beautiful. If she had Indian blood, that would explain her being defensive.

It would be a sorry thing, he thought, if Gibney married her and then later learned the stories were true. He figured the editor would stand by her but would never be able to handle such a truth, given his fine and proper upbringing.

Hank closed his eyes. He thought of the Comanche, Apache, Arapaho, Kiowa, Cheyenne, Sioux, and other tribes, all fighting to be rid of the white invaders. The town was full of people who likely had suffered in the frontier wars. If it was ever proved that Rosalee had Indian blood, she would be scorned and hated.

Still, Gibney could be right. Her high cheekbones and sultry beauty could have resulted from another heritage. The rumors could have been born of jealousy.

Hank fell asleep despite the pain of his wounds.

*   *   *

While Hank slept, there was a meeting in the office of the Silver Palace Saloon. The saloon itself was ornate, with gold-trimmed brackets around the big mirror that hung behind the walnut bar. The tables were well oiled. Chairs had fancy tool work on the backs. Two chandeliers with oil lamps hung from the oval, decorated ceiling. In the far corner, near the piano, was a stage behind blue velvet curtains. The office was plush, with paintings on the walls.

Sheriff Smite and a big rancher named Harris Sloan were seated in soft chairs in front of Silas Tanner's huge walnut desk.

Smite was rubbing his thick nose, his big frame uncomfortable in the cushioned chair. He didn't particularly like the swarthy gambler seated so grandly behind his desk. Red of face, with a jutting chin, Sloan was a big man as well.

Tanner leaned back as he spoke. "That lawman won't be so easy to get rid of."

"Whoever shot him had lousy aim," the sheriff said with a grunt.

"Maybe it was you," Tanner suggested slyly.

The sheriff snorted. "I don't miss."

"And the Smith boys didn't do it," Tanner asserted.

"All right," Sloan said, his red face twisted, "since not one of us admits to havin' pulled the trigger on him or Harrington, maybe we oughta go a step further."

"I don't want to know about it." Smite started to stand up.

Tanner frowned. "You sit right there. Wasn't for me, you wouldn't be wearin' that badge. I mustered all them miners to vote for you, so you just hold on till we're finished here."

"What I was thinkin'," Sloan said, "was maybe we oughta do it legal like. I know a man who could take Darringer in a fair fight."

"Who could that be?" Tanner asked.

"Yancy."

"Yancy? He's a bounty hunter." Smite shook his head. "He's lower than dirt."

Sloan shrugged. "Don't sell him short. He's been educated. He's smart. And I seen him in Denver. He took two men, cold."

Tanner grunted. "I heard Darringer took four."

"Stories don't mean anything," Sloan growled. "I seen this with my own eyes. And he's already at the Miners' Hotel."

"You sent for him?" Tanner asked. "Without talkin' to us?"

"That was afore Harrington was killed. But it's just as well," the rancher said. "We don't want Darringer pokin' around where he ain't wanted. We gotta put a stop to it, but it's gotta be fair and square."

Smite folded his big arms. "There's one thing you ain't thought of. If Yancy's also a bounty hunter, there's a few of us who'd better watch our backs."

Tanner grimaced. Sloan bit his lip. The three men fell silent, studying one another, each afraid to speak of his past.

Finally, Smite leaned forward. "Well, we ain't the only ones. The vigilantes can't be very happy about Darringer's bein' here. And boom towns are always full of 'Smiths.' And I been wonderin' about Roan Carter. Where'd he get all his money? That mine of his weren't never that great."

"Never mind Carter," the saloon owner said. "I'm plannin' to marry his daughter."

Sloan laughed. "You? He wouldn't let you near her with a forty-foot pole."

"I got my ways," Tanner said.

Sloan grunted. "I'm expectin' both of you to put in with me on Yancy."

"He might be hard to control," Smite said. "I understand he's plenty mean. And maybe half Comanche."

Sloan leaned back in his chair. "It's too late now. He's on his way here."

The meeting ended, each man leaving with his own thoughts.

On Monday morning, Hank managed to sit up despite his stiff, painful left shoulder. His head still hurt. He moved to the chair by the window and slid the pane upward so he could breathe fresh air. The hotel veranda in front of his room was empty.

The street was busy. Mule trains were lined up in front of the stores and distant freight offices.

Wagons drove up and down. Horses fidgeted at the railings. Men and women hustled about, and children were playing in front of the mercantile. He could see smoke from the distant smelter and sawmill.

And Rosalee was riding into town from the north on her black mare. Life came back to him. He stood up, washed his face, and pulled on his hat. Though the bandages under his shirt were damp and pinching, he felt there was no time for a bath or shave. He wanted to see her.

He walked into the hallway and down the stairs.

As he walked through the lobby, he saw Gibney helping her down from her mare in front of the hotel. Hank went out onto the porch. She was wearing green velvet, and her shining hair was blowing in the slight wind.

"But I was coming over this afternoon," the editor was saying to her.

"And you still may," she said, smiling at Gibney.

She paused at the sight of Hank on the steps. He was conscious of his badge glittering in the morning light.

"Well, Marshal, I see that you're all right," Gibney said. Then he turned to Rosalee, saying, "I'd be pleased to buy you breakfast."

"I've eaten," she told him, "but I would like a cup of coffee."

Gibney took her arm and guided her up the stairs past Hank, who could only stare at her and tip his hat.

As they passed the lawman, she said over her shoulder, "You may join us, Marshal, if you like."

Hank turned and followed them to the dining room. The three of them took a table by the window, with Rosalee seated between the two men. A thin little waiter brought them coffee, and Hank also had breakfast. As he ate, he listened to small talk without comment.

Gibney cleared his throat. "Uh, Marshal, I have some news for you that cost me a whole dollar."

"Was it worth it?" Hank asked.

"Judge for yourself." The editor reached inside his coat pocket, drew out his newspaper, and handed it to Hank, who laid it on the table.

Rosalee leaned forward to read it as well.

The headlines read FEDERAL MARSHAL MURDERED. The accompanying story offered few details. There was also a story about Hank's being shot. But another item at the bottom of the page had the headline WHY IS YANCY HERE?

"Stumpy sold me the story," Gibney said. "He's the town character. You'll recognize him easy—squashed-in face, bum leg. Anyhow, you can't say I don't take chances."

Rosalee frowned. "That's not taking chances—that's asking to be shot."

"Never knew a gunfighter who wasn't hungry for publicity," Gibney argued.

"But he's a killer," she pointed out. "And a bounty hunter. He won't like your announcing his presence."

Gibney smiled. "Are you worried about me?"

"Yes," she admitted, resting her hand on his arm.

Hank read the article through, noting it gave little information about the bounty hunter and didn't accuse him of anything. It just recited his reputation. Still, publishing it was a brave thing for Gibney to have done.

Suddenly feeling guilty that he had driven the editor to taking chances, Hank leaned back uneasily. Gibney was competing with him, trying to impress this woman.

"You can have the paper for a souvenir," Gibney told him.

Hank shook his head. "No, thanks. I've been shot before."

"I'll take it," Rosalee said. "And if I were you, Marshal, I would find some other town."

"Because of Yancy?" Hank asked.

"No, because these people don't care how they get rid of you."

"Your father included?" Hank inquired.

She stiffened. "I was thinking of the Smiths."

"Have you always lived with your father?" Hank asked.

"For the last three years," she said. "He sent for me when he built the house."

Hank persisted. "What do you know about his past?"

Rising with a frown, she said, "I don't appreciate your questions, Marshal."

Hank stood up to face her, while Gibney stared at them. "Rosalee," the editor said quickly, "one of the reasons I was coming out to see you this afternoon was to ask you to the dance on Saturday."

Still glaring at Hank, she answered, "I would love to go to the dance with you, Nelson."

"Thank you," the editor said.

The tension between her and Hank was still building. She tried to get around him, but he blocked her path, saying, "Just tell me one thing."

"And what is that?"

"That you'll save a waltz for me."

"You? A waltz?"

"Well?" Hank persisted.

"Marshal, if you are still alive and can possibly waltz, I will save one for you."

Gibney smiled. "You'll embarrass yourself, Marshal."

"No one will be looking at me," Hank said.

She caught the compliment and her face flushed with color. He stepped aside, and she hurried off through the lobby.

Gibney frowned. "You're wasting your time."

Hank only grinned. As he watched the newspaperman hurry after Rosalee, he had the strange feeling that she had come into town to see him and not Gibney. Maybe that was wishful thinking.

His grin faded. Suddenly he had realized that now, in addition to avenging his cousin, he had to be concerned about Yancy too. He knew about the bounty hunter who didn't care how he brought men back. He also knew the man was a fast gun for hire.

When he moved out into the sunlight he saw that Rosalee's mare was still tied to the railing. Maybe she had gone to the newspaper office with Gibney.

He crossed over to see the doctor.

With his wound freshly dressed and new bandages under his shirt, he then went downstairs for a shave. The barber talked nonstop and never seemed to hear Hank's interruptions. Hank was glad when he got back on the street.

An excited boy ran past him, yelling, "The stage was robbed back down the river! Everyone was killed!"

Hank watched the boy run across to the hotel. Then he turned and walked over to the stage depot.

Smite came charging out, pausing to glare at Hank. "I'm gettin' up a posse. You comin'?"

"No, thanks."

People were crowding around the depot. Across the street, Gibney and Rosalee followed Stumpy Potts, who had apparently spread the news.

A woman was sobbing inside the stage office.

Gibney hurried over to Smite to get the story. Listening, Rosalee stood back in the crowd.

"The driver lived long enough to tell what happened," Smite told the editor. "He didn't see their faces, but he figured all four of 'em got shot bad. They killed the guard and shot the driver, and the horses went wild. Then the stage rolled over the embankment, down into the river. The passengers, two men and a woman, were killed."

Gibney was writing this down. As Smite called for a posse, Hank kept walking toward the livery.

Then he heard Rosalee call him, and he stopped.

"Aren't you going with them?" she asked.

He turned slowly, seeing the distress in her face. "No."

"But you're a lawman."

"So is Smite. Let him do his job. I've got mine."

"Where are you going now?"

"To check on my horse."

For some reason, she kept following him. In the livery, he walked to the stall where his stallion was standing. It was pawing the sawdust and shaking its elegant head. Its coat was well groomed and glistening black.

Hank turned and saw awe on Rosalee's face.

"He's beautiful," she said.

"I'm taking him for a ride. Want to show me the country?"

She hesitated. "My father would be furious."

"So would Gibney."

A pretty smile crossed her lips. "I'll get my horse."

He watched her walk back into the sunlight. He realized suddenly that he had held his breath and his heart was pounding. He calmed himself and groomed his stallion, then saddled it.

"You're crazy," the livery owner said, coming

forward. "You go riding with her, Roan Carter will kill you."

"Why?"

"He's got big plans for her. Anybody shoots off his mouth around her, he has 'im beat to a pulp. He wants her to marry some fancy man like Gibney. And he won't take kindly to seein' his daughter ridin' with a rebel lawman."

Suddenly Hank heard someone roar with rage. He turned, his hand on his holster. The big, hairy Smith brother was blocking the sunlight in the doorway. The man was a giant, breathing hard and loud. "Marshal, you busted my brother's jaw. Now he can't even eat!" he snarled.

"He asked for it."

Sweating, the livery owner quickly disappeared out the back door of the huge barn. Hank glanced around. Farther back were horses in stalls. Where he stood with his stallion, there were sacks of grain on his right and hay stacked on his left. Two long-handled forks leaned against the wall near several piles of manure.

Smith lumbered forward. His arms were as big around as trees, and his body was huge. His eyes were gleaming in the light that came down through the roof cracks.

Hank turned his stallion, sending it toward the back of the barn. He stood with his hands at his sides. He was a good hand-to-hand fighter, but this man was massive. If Smith ever got his arms around the lawman, Hank would be a goner.

"Marshal, I'm gonna break you in two!"

"You can't count that high."

With a roar, Smith charged like a lumbering bear. Hank jumped aside and tripped him. The big man stumbled and crashed into the nearest manure pile. With a loud growl, he got to his feet, his clothes damp and dirty.

Snarling, Smith came charging again. Hank ducked and stepped aside, hitting him in the gut with his fist. Doing so hurt his hand, since the man's belly was hard as a rock. Smith staggered past, losing his balance. Then he recovered, spun, and grabbed at Hank, who leaped aside again. Smith roared and rushed him. Hank jumped out of the way, slamming his fist into the hairy face and hitting what felt like stone.

Frustrated, Smith grabbed one of the forks and stood with it aimed at Hank. His eyes were wild. "I'll pin you down!"

He threw it hard. Hank jumped aside as it whistled past. The blades jammed into the grain sacks, the handle bouncing wildly for a moment. Hank reached for it but stopped because there was no time. Smith had grabbed the other fork.

Smith came at him like a locomotive, the blades aimed straight at Hank, who drew a deep breath and jumped aside at the last moment.

Unable to stop, Smith collided with the other fork and roared as it jammed into his middle, powered by his own speed. The fork nearly went through him. Gasping for air but trying to rise, the giant fell to his knees. Then he went down on his elbows, doubled up, and rolled on his side. Breathing hard, Hank stood back, sweat covering his face and body.

Staring, Rosalee was on her mare in the doorway.

As the livery owner ran to fetch the doctor to treat the fallen giant, Hank whistled softly. His stallion came forward. Rosalee reined aside as Hank led the animal into the sunlight, its black hide gleaming. He mounted, knowing he had been lucky. If Smith had taken hold of him, he would have had a broken back.

He glanced back at the crowd still at the depot.

Rosalee didn't smile as she rode on past, and he followed, wondering if she was afraid to let the town know they were riding together.

It was late morning, cloudy and cool. The wind was in their faces. They passed the freight office, avoiding a mule train loaded with supplies and iron rails that dragged behind them. A lone rider was hustling them along.

The road wound upward through the hills. On the far right, he could see the smelter. An ore wagon was unloading. Beyond the smelter was the sawmill, smoking away. Farther ahead up the trail, they could see another mule train, each animal carrying a long board on its pack. The ends of the planks were bouncing on the ground.

"Those boards will be a foot shorter by the time they get up there," he remarked.

Rosalee turned from the main trail and headed south through the hills overlooking town. She reined up on a rise to point westward toward a mansion that was surrounded with green aspens. It was big and white with many gables, set on a hill to overlook the town and sloping terrain.

"That's where I live," she said.

"Just you and your father?"

"And three servants."

They rode deeper into the hills now, skirting her home and heading toward the forest that climbed toward the mountains. She was a good rider and had a gentle hand.

Overhead, a red-tailed hawk screeched and spread its great wings across the blue of the sky. Circling only once, the hawk sailed away toward the mountains. They watched until it was out of sight.

At the edge of a crevice that was at least ten feet deep, Rosalee reined to a halt, pointing to a dead, barren oak on the far side, its thickest limb still tied with a piece of dangling rope.

"One of the hanging trees," she said.

Hank twisted about, surveying the terrain. They were surrounded by thick woods and the heavy forest just ahead. He could see only the white tips of the Rockies against the cloudy sky. Then he felt a chill.

The sudden whistle of a bullet past his ear and the report of a rifle startled him. His stallion crashed against her mare, and both mounts headed down into the ravine.

Chapter Three

*R*osalee nearly fell from the saddle as they rode wildly down into the ravine and then reined up.

Hank swung down from his saddle, pulling his Winchester with him. He hit the ground hard, then spun about to catch her arm as she dismounted. Her eyes wide, she dropped to the loose dirt, then stumbled over to press up against the dirt wall of the ravine.

Hank climbed a little, viewing the surrounding area. His heart was in his throat. Though not afraid for himself, he didn't want Rosalee hurt. Watching and waiting, he stared at the surrounding woods.

Abruptly, a dark horse darted through the distant woods and quickly disappeared. Hank was grim, but he finally relaxed, lowering his rifle. He turned to look at Rosalee.

From the purse at her waist, she had drawn a small Smith & Wesson revolver. She looked at him fearfully.

"It's all right," he assured her. "I saw a horse headin' over the hill. He's gone."

43

She hesitated, finally sliding her weapon back into her purse.

There was something intimate about their both being pressed up against the dirt wall, just a few feet apart. Hank couldn't move. She gazed at him a long moment, her lips parted. Warmth radiated from her.

Then she abruptly straightened. He swallowed hard as she moved from the wall. She walked to her mare, then paused and turned to look at him. She would need help mounting.

"If you will give me a lift," she said, "I'll ride home. You can find your way back."

He set his Winchester against the wall and came forward.

She waited, expecting him to help her mount. Her back was to him when he said gently, "First time I kissed a girl, I was seventeen. Her old man grabbed me and threw me in the creek. Then he stomped on me with both feet."

She turned slowly, a soft smile on her face. "Did you see her again?"

"I figured it just wasn't worth it."

Leaning against her mare, she gazed at him thoughtfully.

He stood with his hands at his side, yearning to hold her. He sensed that she liked him. They were but a foot apart. He didn't want to frighten her, and yet he had to try.

He held out his hand. She hesitated.

Then slowly, she straightened. He came still

closer, and she slid her hands into his. He was anxious, certain she could hear his pounding heart. Her fingers were soft and slender, and her very touch sent a thrill down to his boots.

Carefully he leaned forward until his lips rested on hers in a gentle kiss that sent shivers down his back as her lips responded to his.

They drew apart, both too shaken to speak. Out of breath, she shyly cast her gaze to the ground and turned to her mare.

He bent to make a step with his hands, and she mounted, her face flushed with color as she looked down at him and said, "Marshal, please leave my father alone."

Hank was shattered. He felt that her kiss had been only a desperate attempt to save her father, but from what? His stunned look caused her to flinch.

Abruptly, she spun her mare about, riding up the crevice. The animal fought the soft dirt but managed to get to solid ground and into the green grass once more.

Hank took up his Winchester and mounted his stallion, which leaped up the bank, following Rosalee out into the bright sunlight. She reined up not far away, hesitant about the ambush.

"It's all right," he said.

With a toss of her long, gleaming hair, she set the mare into a lope and headed back through the woods. Hank watched her go, then followed at a distance until he was certain she was safely on her way to the mansion. She turned her mare up the road to her home without looking back.

He returned to search for spent shells, finding none. He saw signs of a horse, but the tracks were nondescript, disappearing on the main trail with the multitude of hoofprints. He then decided he would ride up to the diggings.

Meanwhile, her kiss was still soft on his lips. Her plea still rang in his ears.

While Hank rode upward toward the mines, Rosalee hurried her mare up the path leading to the mansion. She was still shaken and couldn't believe she had kissed the lawman.

At the railing, she surrendered her mare to Old Tom, a ruddy-faced handyman with white hair and ready smile. He had been with her father for many years.

Her face warm and flushed, she hesitated. Hints around town had made her believe her father might be wanted by the law. Hank's questions back at the hotel had not left her thoughts.

"Tom, you've known my father a long time, haven't you?"

"Sure have, Miss Rosalee. Why, we were soldiers together."

"Was he ever in any trouble?"

"Any man with as powerful an urge to succeed as your father, why sure, there's been trouble. But he's won out every time, Miss Rosalee. That's why he's got this fine house and you."

"Of course," she said awkwardly.

Turning, she headed up the path, berating herself for even thinking her father could be in any kind of trouble with the law. Yet she had really known him for only three years.

Her father had left to fight in the Civil War when she was small. Her mother had died before the war was over. Devastated by the news, her father had not returned, instead heading west to make his fortune. She had been sent to school in Philadelphia, and he had sent for her only three years earlier.

Climbing the grand steps, she remembered how thrilled she had been with this house. She didn't understand her father, however. He was stern and sometimes harsh, as he was now when he confronted her in the plush parlor. He was biting his pipe stem, his blue eyes narrowed.

"Where have you been?" he demanded.

"Riding."

"Alone?"

"Yes, but—"

He strode forward and grasped her arm. "Your face is flushed. What's happened?"

She freed herself and sat on the soft pink sofa.

"If you will calm yourself, Father, I will tell you."

He looked grim as he sat next to her. "Well?"

"I went into town."

"Why?"

"To look at some satin."

"And?"

"The sheriff was getting up a posse. The stage was robbed and overturned. No one survived. Four men did it."

"So they got the shipment."

"Unless it went into the river," she said, surprised he was thinking only of gold and silver. He seemed to have forgotten the lives that were lost, since he wasn't even asking for names.

"Then you came right back?"

"Well, I showed the marshal some of the country."

"You went riding with that gunfighter?"

"We were both riding in the same direction."

He reached over and gripped her arm. "You listen to me, Rosalee. I don't want you around a man like that. You stay with Gibney, or I'll send you back to school."

"But he didn't hurt me."

"Then why is your face so red?"

She thought quickly. "Well, we were shot at."

He was furious even as he released her arm. "That does it. You don't go riding by yourself, not anymore."

"But, Father—"

"There's a wild streak in you, Rosalee. I wish I could drain that Cheyenne blood right out of you."

She held her head high. "What about Mother?"

He slowly sank back, his hand on his pipe. "She was so beautiful," he murmured, "but she had that same wildness. I just want everything for you, Rosalee. I want you to be a lady and marry a gentleman. I want—"

She put her arm around him and said, "I know, Father. Don't worry. I'll be nice to Gibney."

He turned to hold her, but there were tears in her eyes that he didn't see.

He was her only kin. Rosalee knew she had to do as he asked. And she knew he was right about the gunfighter. She had been attracted, but it was all wrong, a young woman's foolishness.

When Gibney came that afternoon, she was extra nice.

They strolled through the garden behind the house. Red and pink roses were blooming there. She and Gibney sat on a white bench on the sweet-smelling lawn. Because of the cloudy sky, she wore a heavy wool wrap.

"Nelson, do you miss being back East?" she asked.

"Sometimes. But it's so crowded there. I like being able to look from town to the mountains. Someday I'll build a house up here just as grand as your father's."

"You really want to stay here?"

Gibney was suddenly anxious. "Rosalee, if you were ever to say yes, I'd take you anywhere you wanted to go. If you want New York or Philadelphia, it's yours. I just want you to be happy."

She could tell he wanted to kiss her, but she held back. Her lips were still warm from Hank's kiss in the ravine just a few hours earlier.

A young woman's foolishness, she reminded herself. Here was this devoted man her father had chosen. She had to admit she liked the editor quite a lot.

Now he slowly moved toward her and gently, carefully kissed her cheek. She smiled at him. Maybe someday she would learn to love him. And all the while she knew her father was watching from the window.

While Rosalee was being carefully chaperoned, another daughter was sitting in a big room with her father, far out on the lower hills in a rambling ranch house. A fire was still burning in the great stone hearth.

Melanie was sitting next to Harris Sloan on the sofa. She glanced around the room with its horn chair, hides on the floor and walls, and the one cherished piece of furniture, a rosewood piano.

"Papa, don't you ever long to see San Francisco?" she asked.

"What for?"

"Seems like all I know is Denver and St. Louis and this house. And so few single women to talk with."

"What about Rosalee?"

"She has her nose in the air. The ladies don't like it, Papa. And you know, they're sure that Rosalee's got Indian blood. Wouldn't it be terrible if it was true? That would certainly bring her down off her high horse."

"Melanie, don't think like that."

"Why, Papa? You used to fight Indians, remember? Like the ones that killed my mother."

"That was my fault, honey. Denver was isolated by the Cheyenne. We should have stayed with you, but your mother was so all-fired anxious to get to Dodge to see her sister, who was sick and dying. As you know, we went with some wagons and got hit pretty bad. I'll never forget the day I had to bury her."

"So how can you even be nice to Rosalee?"

"Because we don't know the story is true."

"I wish we were away from here, Papa. I want to see stores full of pretty dresses, not just sunbonnets and canvas and bolts of cloth. I'll grow old and wrinkled here, I just know it."

He reached over and hugged her, his red face losing its color. She slid her arm around his neck, longing to find herself anywhere but in the town of Prospect.

Hank couldn't get Rosalee out of his mind. Even as he rode up into the diggings, he was thinking of her.

He worried that she pretended to be interested in him only to protect her father. But who was he to try to take her away from an educated man like Gibney, anyhow? What could Hank Darringer offer but the life of a lawman? He'd be constantly on the trail. She'd be alone, never knowing if he was alive.

Up at the diggings, he saw mines for miles in every direction. Some were just pits in the walls, dirt trailing out. Others were built up with elaborate sluices. The hills were rugged, with a lot of thick brush and juniper.

From here, he could see the town and river far below. He could also see the Carter mansion. Beyond the town, green hills rolled away toward the distant prairie.

"No one admits to anything," a burly miner called Hogan said. "But if anybody here steals from a sluice, you usually find him strung up the next mornin'."

"No one waits for the sheriff?" Hank asked, leaning on the pommel of his saddle.

The miner laughed. "Wait for Smite?"

"Does he ever come up here?"

"Nah. Probably figures he'd get shot."

"You know anything about Marshal Harrington?"

"Well, he come up here all right. He was lookin' for some feller named France. Nobody could tell him nothin'."

Hank thanked him and rode back down the trail.

It was evening when he reached the main street once more. He reined up in front of the freight corrals where wagons were being unloaded. A husky man with no hair was lifting sacks as if they were pebbles. His helper was a short, wiry younger man whose beady brown eyes kept a watch on Hank.

When he saw Hank, the husky man came over.

"Marshal, we was wonderin' when you'd be stoppin' by. This here's Rickles; he helps me out now and then. I'm Pete McCoy. And we don't know nothin' about Harrington, if that's what you wanta know."

"Did you see the stage robbed when you were coming up the road?"

"Nope, but you might as well forget that. They've already hanged 'em."

"What?"

"The posse found them hidin' out and hanged 'em."

"Did Smite try to stop them?"

"Are you loco? These people don't listen to anyone when they're mad. All four had been shot up and couldn't have gotten away, no how."

Hank shook his head, but McCoy shrugged.

"Don't worry about it, Marshal. It's too late."

"Seems to me it would be in your best interest to bring about some law and order in this town."

"Well, sure. We've been robbed a few times ourselves. But a lot of the bad ones come from out of town, Marshal. Like that Yancy fella, sittin' big as day over in the Silver Palace. Got everybody nervous. He's a bounty hunter, you know."

"You worried?"

McCoy grinned. "I ain't sayin', but I figure there's maybe ten people in this town got nothin' to worry about, and they're all female."

Hank had to grin back. Then he sobered as he

looked at the beady-eyed Rickles, who turned and walked away toward the sheds.

"Rickles ride in with you?" Hank asked.

"Nope. Met me here about an hour ago. Why?"

"Someone took another shot at me, up in the hills."

Hank turned his stallion about and rode on to the livery. He put his horse in the stall, unsaddling and grooming it as he listened to the livery owner brag about the hanging.

"It was them all right. We followed their tracks," the owner told him.

"You got a tracker here?"

"Yancy led the way. He's got a surefire nose for it. He's half Comanche, or so they say."

Winchester in hand, Hank left the livery, more uncertain than ever. He had been shot at twice from ambush. He'd run into the Smith brothers. His left shoulder was still mighty sore. And he was no closer to finding out who killed Harrington.

Grim, he went back to the doctor's office. Bandages were removed from his head and replaced on his shoulder.

"You got a mighty dangerous profession," the doctor said. "And one of these days, some fool like Yancy will shoot you down in the street."

"Seems everyone's met this Yancy."

"You'll find him over in the Silver Palace."

"What's your figurin' about him?"

The doctor shrugged. "He's a man who likes to kill."

Hank left the doctor's office and went out into the dark. As he walked down the street along the river, he could hear the happy roar of the white water. He went to the rocky bank, looking down at it in the moonlight.

After a peaceful moment, he walked on to the Silver Palace Saloon. Inside, he found a dozen men seated about the tables. Most were miners. Behind the bar with the pink-faced bartender was a blond woman in red feathers. Maybe thirty years old, she wore a lot of makeup and looked bored.

"What'll it be, mister?" she asked.

"Yancy around?"

"You mean that bounty hunter? He left."

"Was he here this afternoon?"

"Except when he went out with the posse."

The burly bartender looked annoyed at the questions.

"Tanner in?" Hank asked.

"Sure," she said. "Want me to get him?"

Hank shook his head and walked over to the office door, but he didn't knock. He opened it and walked right inside the fancy office. Startled and angry, Tanner was seated at the desk. "What are you doing here, Marshal?" he demanded.

"I'm looking for Yancy."

Hank took a chair and spun it around so he could sit with his back to the wall. Seated, he looked over the plush office. Paintings on the far wall depicted soldiers in gray.

Tanner followed his gaze. "You figure it right,

Darringer. I rode with the Confederacy. Reckon you were too young. Folks don't forget too easily. Now take that Roan Carter, he hates rebs."

"And you hate Yankees?"

Tanner grinned. "Are you askin' if I killed Harrington?"

"Maybe. Or paid the Smith brothers to handle it."

"Listen to me, Marshal. I don't hire men to kill. And I don't need to back shoot any man. I could take you, if I had a mind."

"Were you in on lynching those four men?"

"What lynching? We had a trial and then hanged 'em."

Disgusted, Hank went back into the saloon, closing the door behind him. It was then he saw a new face at the bar.

A dirty man in buckskin, with straggly black hair and a square face with high cheekbones, was leaning on the bar and fingering his drink. He looked mean as a grizzly. The man wasn't overly tall, but he had big shoulders. He was carrying a Sharps buffalo gun and a sidearm that Hank couldn't see.

Slowly Hank approached the bar and rested his left arm on it. Just as slowly the man with the Sharps turned to look at him, smiling with a sneer. The dirty man had small black eyes. His buckskin hat was pulled down on a wide, creased forehead, and he smelled of sweat.

"What are you doing here, Yancy?"

"So you know my name. And I know yours," the man said in a deep, educated voice with a Spanish accent. Coming from this dangerous, savage man, his cultured voice sounded strange.

"What's your business here?" Hank asked.

"My business is bounty, Marshal. This town is a real huntin' ground. I could stay here a long time."

The two men looked each other over carefully.

Hank decided that whatever this man was, he was not a hide-in-the-woods back shooter—at least not one who would hit and run. This man would finish the job.

"You need men like me, Marshal. There's not enough of you, and too many like Smite."

Hank turned, moving away from the bar, his skin crawling. He told himself Yancy would not back shoot him. All the way into the street, he kept telling himself that, over and over, until he was safe and in the clear. Sweat was running down his back.

Then he turned and went up the street, turning right toward the hotel. He was hungry and weary. The Eatery was going strong, so he walked over to it. He found a seat alone with his back to the wall. Hattie was cheerful as usual.

Hank finished his meal and stood up, then stopped cold.

The mean-eyed, skinny-nosed Smith was standing in the doorway, hands at his sides. His anger had turned his face red. He looked more dangerous than his brothers. The other diners suddenly jumped from their seats, some ducking down behind tables.

"Marshal, you busted my kid brother's jaw. And you put my big brother in bed with a hole in his gut."

Hank stood quiet, waiting. He didn't know how fast this man was, but it was obvious Smith was a cold-blooded killer. There was heavy silence in the room. Sweat beaded on Hank's brow. As fast as he was, he never knew if someone else would be faster.

"Marshal, I'm gonna kill you."

"Tanner payin' you?"

"This is my play, Marshal."

Hank waited. Smith spread his feet apart. Death was in his eyes. Smith moistened his lips, waiting as his anger built up. His hands worked at his sides.

Hank's throat was so dry it hurt. He didn't want to kill another man. He didn't want to die. Yet it was either his life or Smith's. He felt his gut tighten.

Smith bent forward slightly. He was snarling. Suddenly, he grabbed for his six-gun.

Hank drew lightning-fast, fanning the hammer and firing before Smith could pull the trigger. Wide-eyed and amazed, a bullet in his heart, the killer staggered back a step. Without firing a shot, Smith crumpled against the doorframe, head down.

"Did you see that draw?" someone whispered.

Hank drew a deep breath. The room smelled of gunsmoke. He slowly holstered his Colt. Angry at having had to kill a man, he just walked over the body and out into the street.

He was still alive, but this town was getting mighty dangerous. And he was no closer to finding his cousin's killer.

The next few days in town were no more productive. A new red Concord stage came in with some eager prospectors who rented horses to get up to the mines. The stage then left with another express shipment of gold and silver, accompanied by two extra guards.

Hank took rides into the hills. No one took another shot at him. He was increasingly nervous, however, and sweat a lot whenever he was out there. There were no further challenges from the Smiths. The sheriff continued to be unfriendly. Yancy was nowhere to be seen during the day, but was always at the Silver Palace at night.

The one exception occurred on Saturday afternoon when Rosalee and her father came to town in a wagon, driving up the street toward the hotel. The sun was bright, making her black hair shine like satin. A light breeze stirred her long tresses about her lovely face. Even wearing her riding clothes and sitting on the old spring wagon, she was a beautiful sight.

As Hank walked from the hotel, Yancy was coming out of the sheriff's office across the street. Yancy stopped dead in his tracks, staring at the young woman with the flowing black hair. He looked stunned as he slowly wet his lips and narrowed his dark eyes. His whole manner changed, as if he were about to take desperate action.

Hank didn't like that look. He met the Carters in front of the hotel. Rosalee allowed him to help her down, but she avoided his gaze. Her father was carrying a carpetbag probably containing her dress for the dance.

"You'd best get inside," Hank told her.

"Something wrong?" Roan Carter asked, joining them.

"Yancy has just seen your daughter," Hank said.

Slowly the Carters turned and looked across the street at the dirty, buckskin-clad bounty hunter. Yancy was standing still, his hand resting on his Sharps rifle. The busy street was full of passing people who were unaware of the look on Yancy's face. Wagons rolled by. An old man on a mule slowly moved in front of Yancy, then turned toward the saloons.

Stumpy Potts came around the corner and stopped cold, staring. Smite was standing in his doorway, curious at Hank's stiff posture. The look on the bounty hunter's square face was more than a look. It was a dangerous leer.

Rosalee stood a moment, transfixed by the man's stare. Her lips suddenly quivered, and she turned and walked up the steps. Carter followed, hurrying her into the doorway.

Hank stood on the steps, watching Yancy and waiting.

Slowly, Yancy stepped into the street, crossing toward Hank, who slowly walked to meet him.

They avoided a passing wagon, then paused, ten feet apart.

Hank studied the fierce-looking man, knowing how many men he had likely killed. The bounty hunter had been all over the West, dragging in the wanted or hauling in their bodies. This sinister man shouldn't be in the same town with Rosalee Carter.

Yancy was looking at Hank with the same obvious disdain, his square face defiant, his dark eyes narrowed. His low, deep voice rose as he expressed his yearning. "That your woman?" Yancy asked. "She looks Indian."

"Spanish."

Yancy moved a step closer. Hank held up his hand as he spoke, his voice clear and forceful: "One more step, and I'll blow your head off."

Chapter Four

*U*nnoticed by anyone but the Carters, Stumpy, and Smite (who had just appeared at his doorway), Hank and Yancy stood in the street only ten feet apart.

Yancy's smile was more like a sneer, his Spanish accent thickened as he said, "I'm in no hurry, Marshal."

"You get anywhere near her, you're a dead man."

Yancy shouldered his rifle. "Our time will come, Marshal."

Hank stood tall and ready, his badge gleaming in the clouded sunlight. His right hand hovered near his Colt.

The bounty hunter looked past Hank to the doorway of the hotel, where Rosalee and her father were standing. He smiled, touched his buckskin hat, and turned about, heading for the river and the saloons.

Hank drew a deep breath. He didn't know if he

was faster than Yancy. He only knew that that man was getting nowhere near Rosalee Carter.

When Yancy was out of sight, Hank looked toward Smite, but the sheriff had retreated into his office. Stumpy hobbled off toward the barber's. Slowly, Hank turned around and looked up the steps of the hotel.

Carter had his arm about his daughter. She looked pale. For a time, she just stared at Hank. Then she allowed her father to turn her around, and they disappeared inside.

Hank shook his head. If Yancy ever laid a hand on Rosalee, Hank would kill him. That was a terrible thing to know about himself.

Now he reflected that he was dirty and sweaty, just like Yancy. He went up to his room and arranged for a bath and a shave.

In the small room just down the hall from his, he sank down deep in the hot water. He was still wearing his hat, but the rest of his clothes lay heaped on a chair. His Colt and holster were hanging on the chair back, just within reach. Soaping himself, he felt good all over.

It was then the door opened unexpectedly.

Rosalee was standing there with a towel. She stared at him as he sat frozen in the dark, soapy water. The tub's high sides hid most of him. All she could see was the upper half of his hairy chest, the bandage still on his shoulder. Yet he felt as if he had been stripped in front of her.

He gaped at her, unable to move.

Suddenly, she laughed. It was a pretty, musical laugh.

"Get out of here," he growled.

"They told me it was my turn," she said, moving forward.

"Get away!"

She paused, delighted with his predicament.

"You should have locked the door," she said.

"I did!"

"Then the lock is broken. I'm glad I found that out before I came in here."

"Get out of here."

"You know what I think?" she mused. "You should take your hat off."

"If you don't get out of here, I'll get up."

She laughed again. "I doubt that. Your face is red."

He sank down deep in the water, exasperated.

"I'm sorry I saved your hide," he growled.

"From that bounty hunter?"

"He's half Comanche."

She sobered, afraid he might speculate further why a man who was half Indian was so taken with her. All she could do was back away and slam the door behind her as she left.

Tears filled Rosalee's eyes and she hurried to her room, but before she could enter, her father demanded, "Rosalee, what's wrong?"

"Nothing."

He followed her into her room, and she finally

told him what Hank had said. She sat on the bed in tears.

"It's all wrong, Father."

"We're makin' it right, honey. So you get yourself all prettied up. Tonight we're going to the dance and we'll show them that pretty gown I had sent all the way from Paris. And when you marry Gibney, won't nobody open their mouth or look sideways at you."

"I wish it were a hundred years from now."

"Honey—"

"Yes, Father. Someday it won't make any difference. All the bloodshed will be forgotten. Indians will be just like anyone else. But right now, it surely does matter. Yet I'd have given anything to tell the truth."

"Honey, I've seen how women with Indian blood are treated. Other women shun them. Men figure they oughta be in saloons. No one shows 'em respect or wants to marry 'em."

"I know," she whispered.

"But we're not goin' to let that happen."

Carter took her in his arms and held her as she wept. Then he stormed out of the room, angry at himself and the whole world. He needed a drink, but he didn't want to run into Yancy, afraid he would try to kill the man.

Carter knew what it felt like to kill. His mouth was dry. He turned down the hallway toward his room, just as Hank, fully dressed, came out of the bathroom.

They faced each other, Carter angry enough to kill the lawman as well. He knew Darringer was fast, but he might be faster. And the man apparently suspected that Rosalee was part Indian. That was intolerable.

But Carter swallowed his anger and said only, "Marshal, I reckon I have to thank you for keepin' that savage away from my daughter."

"You'd have done the same."

"I thank you for that. I'd buy you a drink, but I'm afraid if I run into him, there'll be trouble."

"I'm not a drinkin' man."

Feeling calmer, Carter continued, "Marshal, maybe you can figure why Yancy's in town."

"He's a bounty hunter. Looks like he could make his living around here for a long time."

"But he hires out. He could be after you."

"Maybe."

"You're a cool one," Carter grunted. "I heard about you and the Smith brothers." He brushed on past and headed for his room.

Hank went down into the lobby. It was already late afternoon. This would be a big night for the town. Women were especially excited about the upcoming dance.

He walked outside and to the Eatery. Hattie chatted with him, describing in glowing terms the dance that would be held in a storehouse behind the volunteer fire department.

"We have other dances," she said, "but there's something' special about the spring dance. Everyone comes. I just hope those grubby miners take baths. I danced with one last year who had ticks and fleas. Yuck."

Hank laughed with her. When he was finished, he went outside into the twilight. Something—curiosity, perhaps—drew him to the newspaper office.

He found Gibney washing his hands in a bowl.

"This ink just never comes off," the editor complained. "I wish I had taken up law or medicine."

"So you're getting ready for the dance."

"Yes. I live out back. Have to clean up. Join me if you like."

Gibney's quarters were cramped but adequate. Hank watched him as he shaved with a long razor. This man was going to hold Rosalee in his arms all evening. Hank's throat was dry, and he felt a queer ache in his heart.

"This is the first time Rosalee's let me take her to a dance," Gibney said. "I couldn't even escort her to church. I think I have you to thank for it. She said yes only because she was angry at you."

"What's a Harvard man doing out here, anyway?"

"Well, after I finished there, I traveled some, down through Kentucky, Kansas, and Texas. Never really knew what I wanted. Jobs for an educated man just didn't exist. When I came here, this paper was for sale. Yes, they had hanged the editor. He had been crying for law and order, and I guess they gave him some."

"And then you saw Rosalee."

"You're right on target, Marshal."

"You ever hear of a man named France?"

"Blast," Gibney said, wiping blood from his chin. "Uh, what's that?"

"France. You ever hear of a man with that name?"

"No, why?"

"Harrington was here looking for a man named France. He killed two men in Dodge City. He's maybe fifty, with gray hair."

"Well, that lets me out," the editor said, turning with a grin. "I'm barely thirty."

"They could have had the age wrong. Blond hair could look gray."

Gibney laughed it off. "Marshal, you're ridin' my tail because I'm taking Rosalee to the dance. She did promise you a waltz, but I don't believe you know the steps."

"Since I won't be dancin' with you, I don't reckon you oughta worry about it."

"By the way, I saw you talking to Yancy. What was that about?"

"He took a shine to Rosalee."

Gibney sobered, his mouth tightening. "He's an ugly man."

"Some are just uglier than most."

Gibney donned his new store-bought suit. It was a little snug, but he didn't care. He was grinning from ear to ear as he buttoned his fancy vest.

"You sure enough look like a dude," Hank said.

Gibney made a face as Hank exited. Not wanting to see Rosalee on the editor's arm, Hank crossed the street and stopped as the sheriff came out of his office, all dandied up.

"I got no time for you, Marshal. Them women are just holdin' their breath, waitin' to dance with me."

Hank turned and headed down toward the Silver Palace. He was just trying to find something to keep him busy before the dance. The thought of a waltz with Rosalee in his arms kept distracting him.

Meanwhile, inside the near-empty Silver Palace, Harris Sloan, wearing his blue Sunday suit, was sitting at a corner table and glaring at Yancy. The dirty bounty hunter was leaning back in his chair with an ugly smile.

"What did you say?" the rancher demanded, his voice low.

"My price has gone up," Yancy replied.

"You said you'd take Darringer for a thousand."

"I want more."

"Forget it. We'll get someone else."

"We have a contract. But I'll take five hundred and the woman."

"What?"

"Five hundred and the woman with the long black hair."

"Rosalee Carter? You're out of your mind."

"That's my price, Sloan. Take it or leave it."

"Yancy, you'd never get away with it. Roan Carter guards her like a bear guards its cub. You'd never get your hands on her."

"Then you'd better make sure I do."

"Carter would hunt you down if it took the rest of his life."

"Then I'll make it a short life," Yancy said.

"She's not for the likes of you—she's a white woman."

"Is she?"

"Yancy, I want no part of it. I'll pay you five hundred or a thousand, and that's it. If you annoy her while I'm around, I'll have to stop you."

"You'll help, my friend. Unless you think you can take Darringer, and we both know you can't. In fact, I'm probably the only one who can. Now I'll go take a bath in her honor."

Yancy continued his ugly smile as he stood up.

Harris Sloan could only stare at him. Yancy pushed his chair aside and turned just as Hank Darringer entered the saloon.

Hank paused, watching the big red-faced man at the table. The man had been mighty thick with Yancy, who merely walked past the lawman with a leering smile.

Slowly Hank moved forward, studying the big man, who looked like a rancher. He pulled a chair around so his back would be to the wall, sat down, and said, "I'm Marshal Darringer."

"Harris Sloan," the man said, looking uncomfortable. "Got a ranch northeast of here."

"Good cattle country."

"Yeah. What do you want, Marshal?"

"I want to know your business with Yancy."

"We were playin' cards, that's all."

Hank glanced at the table. There was nothing on it but two whiskey glasses.

"He has his own deck," Sloan grunted.

"You'd play with another man's deck?"

"Look, Marshal, I got no time for you. I've got to meet my daughter at the hotel. We're getting ready for the big dance."

"You ever been to Dodge?"

" 'Most everybody who's ever been on the cattle trail has been to Dodge."

They both paused as Tanner came out of his office. The gambler had a fine new suit of dark wool and a fancy red vest. He came over to them, smiling.

"I plan to dance with all the ladies," Tanner said.

"Me too," Sloan grunted, getting up and walking out with Tanner.

Alone and thoughtful, Hank sat quietly for a long moment. The painted woman came over, smiling down at him. She had a nice face and clear brown eyes. "My name's Sugar," she said. "Can I get you a drink, Marshal?"

"I don't drink."

She sat down, looking suddenly weary. "Good."

He grinned at her. "Do you work all the time here?"

"They have a hard time keeping women in the

saloon. They make more money at the dance hall, or they get married. Me, I gave up all that hard dancing, because my feet aren't so good."

"What do you know about Tanner?"

"Not much," she said, glancing nervously toward the burly bartender. "And the last woman who shot off her mouth was beat up."

"By Tanner?"

"No one knows for sure." She leaned forward and put her soft hand on his big rough one. "If the barkeep thinks we're gettin' friendly, it's all right for me to talk to you."

He turned her hand in his and leaned forward.

She hesitated, then whispered, "All I know is that he came here from Kansas. He was in some kind of trouble there and can't go back."

"You know what kind of trouble?"

"I don't know."

"Sugar, did you ever meet Marshal Harrington?"

"No, but I saw him. When he first came in here, he was talking to Stumpy Potts. Stumpy's sort of our own built-in telegraph. And speaking of that, did you know they're gonna put in a telegraph line here? Can you imagine that? Next thing, we'll have an opera house. I can sing," she added promptly.

"You sing here?"

"No, 'cause Tanner says my singing's too high-toned. I guess I do hit a few high notes."

"Maybe you ought to head for Denver, give opera a try."

"Maybe I will," she said, her smile weary.

Hank thanked her. He released her hand, tipped his hat, and left the saloon. Outside, it was dark and cold. He wasn't sure he was ready for the dance.

He had learned to waltz, but he wondered if he dared put his arms around Rosalee and whirl her across the dance floor. If he did, everyone in the room would know how he felt about her. They were bound to see it all over his face.

As he turned into the main street, he could see people hurrying toward the fire department. Street lamps and starlight guided them. Women wore their finery. Men wore suits and hats. Some were walking, while others were coming into town by wagon and buggy.

It took Hank a long time to get over to the dance. The old storehouse had been opened up on the south wall and decorated for the occasion. Curtains now hung on the windows, and the hardwood floor and outside platform had been polished. The dancing would be inside where it was warm, or outside under the stars.

Punch and liquor were being served on tables near the front entrance. There was also a lot of food: pots of beans, fat potatoes, sliced venison, biscuits, eggs stuffed with something, cookies, cakes, and lots of pies.

Most of the three hundred people there were dancing. At the far end of the hall, fiddlers were playing a lively reel. He didn't see anyone he knew.

Even the miners had cleaned up, their big boots clunking on the hard floor. Merchants, cowhands, and miners danced with ladies wearing their best clothes. Children were playing in a corner.

Hank helped himself to food and punch.

"Try the apple pie, Marshal," a creaky voice said.

Hank glanced at the little man who had spoken. "You're Stumpy Potts," he said.

"Yeah. Try the eggs too, Marshal."

"I want to talk with you about Harrington."

Stumpy looked around to be sure there was no one in earshot. "It'll cost you, Marshal."

"All right," Hank said, twisting a gold coin in his fingers. "Did you send for Harrington?"

"Well, I maybe wrote a sort of letter to Denver, kind o' hintin' I might know somethin' interestin'. I just hung around the saloon till a Federal marshal showed up."

"What did you tell him?"

"How I saw the Dodge City poster crumpled up in Smite's wastebasket. I got it out, figured it was important, and wrote me that letter."

"Why was it in the wastebasket?"

"I don't know. That's where I was always findin' 'em, and I just figured ol' Smite was too scared to keep 'em."

Hank grimaced at the thought of Smite's method of keeping his job soft and safe. He could also see that Stumpy knew how to make a living in this town.

"You still have the poster?" Hank asked.

"No. And I told the marshal I figured it could be Roan Carter. He was outa town a lot about then. Or Sloan and Tanner, 'counta they got here about three years ago."

"I already knew about them," Hank said, slipping the coin back into his pocket.

"But there's one more."

"You're draggin' me by the tail, Potts. I don't take kindly to your makin' things up."

"I think it's Gibney."

"What?"

"Well, he got here about a year ago, bought the newspaper, and always has money. He's a little too fancy for my taste. He could be that feller France."

"Or the other man. France was supposed to be fifty."

"Well, it was dark when the witnesses saw the marshal and guard shot down. As for Gibney, why's a fancy feller like that holed up in a crummy town like this?"

"Maybe he's on a crusade. You got any idea who's been takin' shots at me?"

"I'll find out, if you want."

"I want."

Hank drew out the gold coin and slid it into Stumpy's greedy hands. The little man hobbled away, pocketing his money.

Hank shrugged and turned to look at the whirling dancers. As the snappy reel continued, they covered the dance floor and spun onto the outside platform. Now he saw Melanie. Wearing a pretty pink dress, she was dancing with her father. Smite was kicking up his heels with a plump little lady.

The dance over, the couples gasped for breath and plopped down on the benches surrounding the room. There was a lot of laughter.

Melanie and her father came over for punch. She smiled at Hank and introduced him to her father, explaining she had met the lawman in church.

"I've met the marshal," Sloan grunted.

"I saved a dance for you, Marshal," she said, looking through her dance card. "Yes, it's the next one."

Hank felt cornered. Luckily, the dance was a slow two-step. Melanie felt soft and supple in his arms, her pink fluffy dress making her look like a little girl. Her blond hair was in big curls draped down her back. She did look mighty pretty. And her smile was infectious.

"Tell me, Marshal, have you ever been to St. Louis?" she asked. When he nodded, she continued, "I just love the big cities, don't you? So much going on there. The ladies all have pretty dresses and—"

A tall, young merchant abruptly cut in. Hank didn't mind, as he felt awkward on the dance floor. He wasn't sure he still remembered how to waltz. The wife of a friend had once taught him to dance, but that was years ago.

As he was heading back to the punch table, he paused.

There in the doorway was Roan Carter, wearing a handsome dark suit. Behind him was Gibney, dressed in his new outfit.

And with the editor was Rosalee.

She was stunning in a shiny green satin dress trimmed with glittering sequins. Though not too low, the dress left her throat and shoulders bare, and she looked like a princess. About her neck was a strand of shining green stones, matching her earrings. Rosalee's black hair still hung loose on her shoulders and down her back. People turned to look at her. Women admired the dress. Men only stared.

Hank couldn't take his eyes off her.

The music started again. Gibney led Rosalee onto the dance floor, and other men followed them, trying to get their names on her dance card.

As she swung into Gibney's embrace, she looked toward Hank. She smiled, but Hank couldn't tell if he was the target.

Everyone wanted to dance with her. Tanner had two turns with her. The saloon owner was graceful and suave. He reluctantly surrendered her to her father, who later handed her to Sloan. Soon she was back in Gibney's arms.

Watching her whirl about, Hank began to wonder how he dared to aspire to this spectacular young woman. Yet when a waltz started later in the evening and she beckoned to him, he rushed to her side.

"I believe this is your dance," she said.

Gibney reluctantly stepped aside. Hank put his right hand at her waist and took her right hand in his left. She smelled delicious, like every flower he'd ever known. Her dark blue eyes were twinkling.

She smiled. "I'm glad you had a bath."

"So am I," he said awkwardly.

"You're a fearsome man. It's good to have you at a disadvantage."

But to his surprise as well as hers, Hank stepped into the waltz with grace and grandeur. They swung with the music, her dark hair flying. She was so beautiful it hurt to look at her.

Bravely he spun her out under the stars. She swayed in his embrace, sometimes so close he could feel her sweet breath on his face. It hurt to think that her only interest in him might be to protect her father.

"Why, Marshal, you dance splendidly."

"Only with you."

Breathless now as they whirled, she kept watching him, her smile increasing as he spun her through the fancy steps he thought he had forgotten. The fiddles were outdoing themselves, their melody sweet and lilting.

As the music stopped, he swept her back into the circle of his right arm. She was out of breath, gazing up at him as if she, too, remembered their kiss that day in the ravine. Her eyes were glistening like stars.

Then she recovered and became formal once more, stepping back from him. Though overly polite, she was smiling as she gave a slight curtsy and said, "Thank you, Marshal."

Before they could go back inside, they heard a scream in the bushes behind the building. There was sound of a scuffle.

Hank spun. He wasn't about to wait for Smite. He ran toward the noise, his hand on his holster. A woman was in trouble. Darringers never stood for that.

He crashed through the brush as a big man spun about, gun in hand. It was the burly bartender from the Silver Palace. Hank rushed him. They grappled and fell in the spiny brush, rolling into the dirt. Powerful arms tried to get around Hank's back. Breath tight, Hank slammed his fist into the man's fat face.

They broke apart, scrambled to their feet, and danced a little, each looking for an opening.

"You gonna arrest me, Marshal? She ain't worth it."

It was then that Hank saw Sugar rising from the brush. Her dress was torn from her shoulder. Her hair was spilling about her battered face. Badly shaken, she collapsed.

Hank was furious. The big man charged him again. Hank jammed his fist into the bartender's belly, jumping aside. The man rushed, and this time, Hank didn't get out of the way. Huge, powerful arms clasped the lawman, lifting him in the air and trying to break his back.

Hank knew he had only seconds. He slammed

his fist into the man's nose, flattening it. Gasping and choking with pain, the bartender fell back and away from him.

"Blast you, Marshal!"

It was almost too dark to see the man draw.

Hank acted mainly from instinct, his gun leaping into his hand and firing. The big man's bullet whistled past his ear.

Sugar cried out as the bartender, swearing, caught at his bleeding chest and fell to his knees. He died before he hit the ground.

Hank slowly holstered his smoking gun. Rosalee came running forward. She hurried to Sugar and helped her stand. Devastated and angry, Rosalee slid her arm about the saloon woman. Sugar leaned on her, surprised.

Another woman, who apparently worked with Sugar, came forward. "It's all right, Miss Carter. I'll take her."

Rosalee watched the women move away. She wiped a tear from her face. Hank watched her. She had never looked more beautiful. They both turned as Smite came over, grumbling that his evening was interrupted.

Still upset, Rosalee started back inside, then froze.

Standing in the hall entrance was Yancy. He was still in his buckskins, but he looked surprisingly clean. His long dark hair had been washed and combed, and his hard face was freshly scrubbed. He was hatless, but he still wore his sidearm.

Now he was moving forward. People stared as Rosalee retreated to Hank's side, taking his arm. Gibney hurried to join them, followed by her father.

Still, Yancy kept coming slowly forward.

Chapter Five

A hush fell in the dance hall. Everyone turned to watch Yancy as he walked toward Rosalee, who was still clinging to Hank's arm. Her father stepped in front of her and walked toward Yancy. The bounty hunter stopped.

"We had better talk," Yancy murmured, "or you'll hang."

Roan Carter hesitated, then nodded. To everyone's surprise, Yancy and Carter turned and walked back into the night.

Rosalee, who had been holding her breath, suddenly sighed and put both hands to her face. Gibney took her arm and led her back onto the floor as the music started. Listlessly she danced with him.

Hank was disturbed. He wanted to follow Yancy and Carter, but he was interrupted by Melanie.

"Why, Marshal, I just happen to have another dance for you."

As they danced, she kept flirting with him. He liked it.

But he kept wondering if Yancy had something on Carter, and how the bounty hunter might use such knowledge. He glanced at Rosalee, who was spinning by in Gibney's arms. She cast a smile his way.

He and Melanie came to a halt as the music stopped.

The four of them met at the punch bowl. Rosalee and Melanie politely complimented each other on their dresses.

Gibney grinned at Hank. "Nice dance, don't you think?"

"It was," Hank said, nodding toward the door.

In walked Roan Carter, followed by Yancy, both coming over to join them. Yancy bowed to Rosalee. Her father's face was void of color, his mustache twitching. The man looked as if he had been shot ten times in the belly, and when he spoke, his voice was hoarse.

"Rosalee," he said, "I'd like you to meet Mr. Yancy. He would like to have a dance with you. I told him you'd oblige."

The group was silent. Rosalee stared wide-eyed at her father, then at Yancy. Acting polite and gentlemanly, the bounty hunter was on his best behavior. When the music suddenly started, he held out his hand to Rosalee.

She hesitated, still staring at her father. She then glanced helplessly at Hank and the ashen Gibney. Yancy offered his arm. She took it fearfully, and he led her onto the dance floor.

Shaken, she held her breath as he put his hand at her waist and began to dance a two-step with her. To her dismay, he was a good dancer. His small black eyes were fixed on her as he swung her about.

"You are Indian," he said in a low voice.

"Spanish," she murmured.

"Indian. You think I would not know one of my own?"

"You're wrong."

"Maybe you have only a few drops, but you are Indian."

"Mr. Yancy, I think this dance is over."

But the music continued, and he refused to let her stop.

"You insult me," she added.

"I want you."

Fear shot through her. Her heart was racing.

"I'm going to marry Mr. Gibney."

"I will tell him the truth. He won't marry you."

"Why are you doing this terrible thing?"

"Because I want you."

Her face was flushed, and there were tears in her eyes. She was frantic, praying to be rescued by someone. She looked up as Hank suddenly cut in, drawing her toward him. Yancy was furious, his hand on his gun.

Hank let his own hand slide downward. "Go ahead, Yancy."

But the bounty hunter slowly relaxed and smiled, his face sinister. "I have had my say, Marshal."

With that, Yancy turned and strutted like a king to the entrance. He disappeared into the night with everyone staring after him.

Rosalee fell into Hank's embrace, allowing him to swing her about as long as the music continued. She was shattered, and tears trickled down her face.

He spun her back under the stars, then off the platform, where he allowed her to stop. She leaned on the fence, one hand on her throat. Hank kept his distance.

"Are you all right?" he asked quietly.

She looked past him at the whirling dancers. The music seemed louder than ever. In the starlight, her distress was obvious. Yet she looked beautiful. "That horrible man," she said shakily.

"What did he say to you?"

She hesitated, looking away. "He was just—awful."

"Rosalee, what did he say?"

"That he wanted me."

"And?"

"That was enough."

"Don't worry. No one in this town will let him come near you."

"My father did. Why did he do that, Marshal?"

"He seems to be afraid of Yancy."

"Like everyone else," she whispered. "Except you."

She looked up at him now. The music had stopped. They seemed very alone out there in the dark. For a moment, he thought she might come to him. He wanted to hold her, comfort her, but he didn't move.

She straightened and took his arm.

Hank led her back inside to her father. Then he stood back, watching the editor take possession.

Gibney was still ashen as he took her hand in his. "Rosalee, are you all right?"

She looked at her father, who avoided her glance.

"I think we should make our announcement," Gibney said, "and put an end to this here and now."

Looking up at Gibney, she hesitated. She wondered how he would react to Yancy's story. She looked at Hank, strong and masterful and suddenly so protective. Where had Gibney been when she had been trapped with Yancy? It was Hank who had been brave enough to rescue her.

Again she looked at her father. He had no color in his face. Now he turned to her, his voice low.

"I'm sorry, Rosalee. Mr. Gibney will see you back to the hotel, I'm sure."

"Father, don't leave," she said.

But he turned away, a bent man who seemed barely able to walk. Hank followed him into the night. On the boardwalk, Carter turned to look at the lawman. "What do you want, Darringer?" he demanded.

"What's Yancy got on you?"

"Nothing."

"You just handed your daughter over for nothing?"

"It was only a dance."

"You let a killer put his dirty hands on her."

"Back off, Darringer, or I'll blow you apart."

They faced each other in the starlight. The music and laughter sounded far away. Both stood with their hands at their sides.

"Go ahead, Darringer. I just don't care."

"I don't plan to fight you, Carter."

"You afraid?"

"I've got my reasons."

"Ah, Rosalee? Stand in line, Darringer. Way back in line, because she's not for you. She's got to marry someone like Gibney. I won't have it any other way."

"I plan to change her mind."

Hearing his own words, Hank was shaken, but he would not back down from his intentions.

"I won't approve of any such thing," Carter said.

"After tonight, your approval don't stand for much."

"I didn't have any choice in there, Darringer."

"I believe that. Now tell me why."

"Go to the devil!" Carter said, spinning about.

Hank stood in the chill of night, watching the man hurry down the street toward the hotel. If Carter was a wanted man and Yancy knew it, Rosalee was in danger. Now Hank began wondering just what kind of man Carter might turn out to be. And if he had ever used the name France.

He went back to the dance but only to watch. When Gibney and Rosalee finally left, he waited a few minutes before following. He kept a respectful distance as the editor walked her back to the hotel.

On the porch steps, she stopped Gibney. He took her hands in his and bent forward to kiss her cheek. Then she entered the hotel in somewhat of a hurry.

Gibney waited a long while, then turned and went back down the steps. He walked toward Hank, who stopped and waited. "Were you following us?" Gibney demanded.

"Yes, I was."

Gibney drew a deep breath. "Yeah, sure, I understand."

His shoulders stooped, the editor walked past him. Hank looked up and down the street. Almost everyone was still at the dance. At least Rosalee was safe in the hotel. Weary, he went into the hotel and up to his room.

Rosalee confronted her father when he joined her in her room. Her face flushed, she sat on the bed, unmindful of her Paris gown. "Father, I don't understand."

Carter sat down and looked at her sadly. "Before I met your mother, Rosalee," he said, "I was in trouble with the law."

"What was it, Father?" she asked, frightened.

"Just a foolish fight over cards. Nothing serious, honey. But I guess Yancy's memorized all the reward posters ever printed, because he knew about me. His only price for silence was a dance with you. What could I do?"

"He was awful, Father. He said I was Indian. He kept saying it. He said even if I had only a few drops, I was Indian."

"He's only guessing, Rosalee."

"Then he said he wanted me."

Carter's face went dark with fury. "I promise you, honey, he's not going to harm you."

"He's a dangerous man, Father. I'm afraid."

"Now, you just go on to sleep, honey. Lock your door, and don't worry."

She stood up with him, and he held her, kissing her cheek. When he was gone, she burst into tears.

The bounty hunter was in his glory. He was waiting near the newspaper office when Gibney returned. He forced his way inside as the nervous editor glared at him. Gibney turned up the lamp and busied himself with newsprint.

"All right, Yancy, what do you want?" he demanded.

"Rosalee."

"You're mad."

"She's got Indian blood."

"That's a lie. In fact, that's slander. If we had any lawyers here about, you could be sued in a court of law."

"Now you know. Now you won't marry her."

"I don't believe your dirty lie. Get out of here!"

Gibney's heart began racing, and he worried he might be shot down this instant. He turned to the type boxes and fiddled with the letters. Unnerved by this fierce-looking man, he felt himself starting to sweat.

"You think you're so fancy," the bounty hunter said. "Well, I had schoolin', just like you."

"No, not like me."

"You stay away from Rosalee, or you're a dead man."

Gibney heard the bounty hunter leave, closing the door behind him. The editor drew a deep breath of relief. Then he slammed his fist down on the type bin, sending the letters flying. His face was drawn, but he told himself grimly that Yancy must be lying.

Rosalee had Spanish blood. She was beautiful. Gibney loved her. She would give meaning and direction to his life. He would take her away from here so the lies would stop.

As Gibney still slammed about his office, Yancy walked into the Silver Palace with his head held high. Tanner and Sloan were not far behind. The three of them met in Tanner's office.

The saloon owner was annoyed with Yancy. "You stay away from Rosalee," Tanner warned him. "I plan to marry her."

"We're not getting anywhere," Sloan snapped. "Forget the girl. Let's talk about getting rid of Hank Darringer before he stumbles onto somethin' he shouldn't. Yancy, you assured me you could take him in a fair fight."

"I'll take care of Darringer," Yancy said, rising. "You just arrange for me to get the girl."

The gunman left, leaving Tanner and Sloan to work things out.

"You figure Yancy knows about us?" Tanner asked.

"Maybe. After he gets Darringer and collects, we had better watch out."

"I'm not letting him put one finger on Rosalee."

"How will you stop him?" Sloan asked.

"You've forgotten. I'm pretty fast with a handgun."

"In a fair fight, maybe. What makes you think Yancy always fights fair? I tell you, Tanner, we got a dangerous man on our hands."

"Let him get Darringer first. Then we'll deal with him."

Sloan shrugged and left the office. He saw Yancy at the bar but continued out into the night. Sloan had more honor in him than Tanner. He hated what they had to do.

Yet he had a lot of land and cattle. He had a daughter. He wanted her to have comfort and wealth, to marry well. He couldn't give up everything he had worked so hard to build. And he didn't want to hang.

Back in the hotel, Hank paced his room. He was certain that the man called France had been Harrington's main target in this wide-open town. France and another man had killed a deputy U.S. Marshal and a guard in Dodge City three years ago, escaping with a fortune.

Stumpy had found the reward poster, crumpled in Smite's basket, and had sent word to Denver. Harrington had come here alone because of Hank's duty to deliver a prisoner to Canon City.

Who had murdered Bob Harrington? France? Who was France?

His cousin Bob had been like the father Hank had lost so long ago. Fury still raged in Hank over Bob's death. He also wanted to know who was responsible for the attempts on his own life. Grimacing, he put his hand on his sore left shoulder and paced some more.

Then he went down the hall to the veranda. Being outside in the cold of night, under the stars, would allow him to breathe, to think clearly. He moved toward the street and paused near the light from a window.

It was then that he realized he was not alone.

At the far end of the veranda, her hands on the railing, was Rosalee. She was wearing a blue cape. Her long black hair shone like satin in the starlight and stirred in the slight wind. She turned, staring at him.

Slowly she walked toward him.

Hank felt terribly awkward. He was so in love with her, he wasn't sure how to handle it anymore.

He told himself she had no true interest in him. But he prayed her father was not France.

She paused a few feet from him. The pale light from the window cast a glow on her lovely face. She was smiling. "I'm glad you're here," she told him. "I couldn't sleep."

"Neither could I."

Her smile faded. "Marshal, I'm afraid."

"Your father will look after you. So will Gibney."

"And you? Will you also be my protector?"

Her voice was soft, almost plaintive. Her dark eyes glistened in the starlight as the breeze lifted her ebony hair. Her face seemed white. The cape hid her lovely form as she leaned on the railing.

Hank swallowed hard. His mouth was dry. How he wanted to reach for her, hold her, and protect her.

"It's my job," he said lamely.

"Has it always been your job?"

"Reckon I always wanted to be a peace officer."

"My father said you had been wanted by the law at one time. He remembers the Darringers were in trouble."

Hank felt a need to explain. "Back in Texas, my brother Clay and I tried to help a widow fight off some carpetbaggers. We both ended up in jail. My brother Ben, he's a lawyer now, he busted us out. We were on the dodge for a couple of years. Had to use different names. But last fall, we got pardons, thanks to Ben. That's when I got this badge."

"So you have two brothers."

"Three. Jess, he follows the trail herds. Haven't seen 'im since last summer. My mother, she lives down in Texas. She was widowed, married another Darringer when we were small. Got some half brothers and sisters. And a few cousins, I reckon."

"And Marshal Harrington?"

"My cousin, but he was like a father to me."

"I'm sorry."

"Are you going to marry that editor?" he asked abruptly.

"My father says I am."

"And you?"

She turned, gazing down into the street. He followed her glance to the burning street lanterns, the dark stores up the street. Across from them, the sheriff's office was dark as well. The night was still, cold, and empty.

And she hadn't answered. He looked at her lovely profile. Her nose was perfect, her throat smooth and white. The wind kept lifting her long, satinlike black hair and brushing it around her face.

Hank persisted. "Are you going to marry him?"

"Unless someone changes my father's mind," she said, still gazing into the street.

Hank drew a deep breath. He didn't know if she was asking him to step into her life, or if she was really forced to do her father's bidding.

After a moment, she spoke again. "It was wonderful at the dance, the way you helped that poor woman. You must be very proud of that badge."

Slowly she turned to gaze up at him. Her soft lips were parted. He remembered how sweet they tasted. She moved toward him. Her soft white hands reached to his rough face. He drew a deep, painful breath.

Standing on her tiptoes, she lifted her lips to his. He shivered down to his boots as their kiss lingered. His hands hung limp at his sides. He just couldn't react. She drew back from him. He swallowed hard.

Then, unable to stop, he moved toward her.

Suddenly, a rifle shot cracked in the night, the bullet whistling where the back of his head had been. The slug crashed into the window behind him, glass shattering. He thought he heard a woman's cry.

At the same instant, he seized Rosalee's arm and threw her back against the wall, where she cowered and dropped to her knees.

Hank leaped from the veranda, dropping crazily down toward the street as the rifle cracked again with a flash of light from the alley between the jail and the barber's.

Chapter Six

*H*ank hit the ground in front of the hotel, barely missing the hitching rail and a nervous sorrel. He instantly rose as the rifle barked again from the alley across the street. The bullet singed his collar.

It was dark except for starlight and the lanterns.

Six-gun in hand, he ran in a crazy pattern toward the alley. The rifle barked again, the bullet cutting through his left sleeve. He dodged and ducked, finally hitting the far boardwalk.

His heels clattered loudly as he crossed it and jammed himself up against the wall of the jail. The alley between him and the barber's was dark, silent. No light came from the jail window.

Hearing the clatter of boots, he darted into the alley just as a figure ran out at the back end. He charged down toward the exit, then halted at the back wall of the barber's. Slowly he peered around the edge of the building.

The rifle cracked again, the bullet cutting the wood as he jerked back. He peered out quickly and saw a figure running up behind the post office and stage depot. He broke into a run. By the time the man reached the back of the express office, Hank was only twenty feet from him.

Frantic because a wagon blocked the next alley, the man spun about, dropping his rifle and pulling his six-gun. As he aimed, Hank fired.

The man jerked back like an empty sack and then hunched over, dropping to his knees. Again the man tried to fire.

Hank aimed but hesitated. The man fell face down in the dirt, rolling on his side. His hat had fallen away.

Cautiously Hank approached. The starlight didn't show much. The man wore average work clothes.

As Hank knelt, men came hurrying around the buildings. The barber was carrying a lantern. The doctor was close behind. Half-dressed, Smite finally appeared.

Hank turned the man over. It was Rickles, the freighter's helper.

The mean-eyed little man gazed up at him, blood running through his fingers as he gripped his right chest and shoulder. Rickles looked frantic, near hysterical, obviously believing his time had come. His gaze was wild and fearful.

"You shoot at me tonight?" Hank asked, kneeling.

The man nodded, unable to speak.

"You shoot at me outside the church?"

Again the man nodded.

"And up near the Carter mansion?"

Rickles coughed, eyes round, but he nodded.

"Who paid you?" Hank persisted. "Who helped you?"

The man lay in agony as the doctor also knelt. The barber held the lantern closer. The doctor pushed the lawman away. After tearing open the man's shirt and leaning down in the poor light, the medic wiped away the blood with a cloth soaked in alcohol.

"Did you kill Marshal Harrington?" Hank asked.

Rickles opened his glassy eyes, shaking his head firmly. At last, he managed to speak. "I'm dyin', Doc," he gasped.

"No, you're not," the doctor said, working on his right chest near the shoulder. "I just have to get the bullet out."

Suddenly realizing he was going to live, Rickles became tight-mouthed and refused even to look at Hank.

The doctor stood up. "Get him to my office."

"And then lock him up," Hank told Smite.

Reluctantly Smite nodded as Rickles got to his feet.

Hank stood up slowly. He saw dislike in the sheriff's narrowed eyes and frowning mouth. He wondered how long it had been since anyone had been in the town jail.

"What happened?" Smite grunted.

"I was on the hotel veranda," Hank said. "He shot at me from the alley next to the jail. Where were you?"

"Asleep. It's long after midnight," Smite reminded him.

The doctor, Rickles, and Smite went back through the alley and down the street toward the medic's office.

Grim, Hank turned his back on the others once he reached the street. On the boardwalk, he saw other men approaching. He ignored them and crossed toward the hotel.

He paused in front, gazing up at the vacant veranda.

Twice Rickles had shot at Hank when Rosalee was with him. That made him furious. She had been put in danger because of his badge. That hurt.

He remembered the shattered glass. Had he heard a woman's cry? Had it been Rosalee?

"Marshal, send the doctor!" Rosalee suddenly called from the veranda. "Hurry! It's Melanie!"

Leaving Smite and Rickles, the doctor quickly crossed over and ran after Hank, who was charging up the steps and into the hotel.

Leaping the steps three at a time, Hank made it to the landing and down the hallway. Out of breath, he saw two older women crowding the doorway to a room near where he had stood on the veranda. They looked horrified.

Hank and the doctor entered to find Rosalee and Sloan kneeling beside Melanie, who lay sprawled on the floor by the window. She was covered with a blanket, her eyes round and filled with tears. Sloan looked stunned. Rosalee's blue cape was splattered with blood.

Hurriedly, the doctor pushed everyone aside and knelt with his little black bag. He drew back the blanket. There was blood on Melanie's neck, and she was breathing hard and painfully.

Rosalee stood up. She was trembling so much that she was barely able to stand. A woman came to take her arm and lead her away. As she passed Hank, Rosalee looked up with tears in her eyes.

Hank saw Sloan's great body shaking badly. His daughter was leaving him all too quickly. The rancher suddenly seized her arm. He was shattered, fearful. "Melanie!" he cried.

And then it was over. Sloan knelt and drew her lifeless body into his arms, hugging her and sobbing. His whole form was quivering.

Hank felt anger rising within him. Maybe Melanie had had foolish dreams, but she had been a lovely young woman. He couldn't run out and smash Rickles, because the man was a prisoner, but he had the fierce and painful urge to do so.

He had to find out who had paid Rickles to shoot him.

Fury drove him out of the room and into the hallway. The two women there had seen Melanie die, and they were holding each other and weeping as they moved down the hallway.

In a silent rage, Hank then followed the doctor

out of the hotel and across the street. Hank waited until he was alone with the sheriff, the doctor, and the prisoner up in the doctor's office.

"You lock him up, Smite," Hank said grimly. "Now it's for murder."

"I didn't kill no one," Rickles snarled.

"Your bullet missed me and hit Melanie Sloan. She just died."

Rickles was aghast. "But I wasn't aimin' at her."

"Yeah," Smite said. "How can you call that murder?"

"It's murder," Hank insisted. "You intended to kill me. That's enough."

Smite looked plenty upset over having to deal with the situation. He stood against the wall, arms folded, as the doctor worked on Rickles' shoulder.

"You got a judge in this town?" Hank asked.

Smite shrugged. "Winslow, our mayor, he's been a lawyer. He's been judge now and then, but I don't know if he can handle this. You might have to take Rickles to Denver for trial."

"We'll hold it here, tomorrow," Hank said.

Rickles was anxious. "Who's gonna be my lawyer?"

"Only fair man I know is Gibney," Hank said. "You want him?"

Rickles hesitated, his mind clicking before he answered. "That newspaper fella? Okay."

And so it was that when Rickles was locked up and Smite was asleep on his bunk, Gibney came to speak with the prisoner, studying him through the bars. They spoke in low murmurs. They were alone with the snoring sheriff.

"You got to get me out of here," Rickles said.

"Listen, her death was an accident. You won't hang for that."

"No, but we'd both hang for what happened in Dodge City."

"Dodge has nothing to do with this."

"If they ever find out your middle name is France, you'll be as dead as me. And it was you shot that marshal and the guard in Dodge, not me. And you got most of the money."

"You gambled your share."

"Five hundred dollars? That wasn't much for all we did."

"I invested my half. So I can help you with some cash to get you on the trail."

"Yeah, well, you'd better get me out of here fast."

"Listen to me, Rickles, and listen good. At the trial, we got to say you never intended to shoot the marshal, that you only wanted to scare him."

"Yeah, but why?"

"Will you just listen to me? I know enough about the law to know that they'll be looking for intent to kill. You just didn't intend to kill him or Melanie Sloan."

"And what if it don't work? Me takin' potshots at Darringer was your idea, not mine. I ain't hangin' alone."

"You'd be hanging for the girl. I didn't do that."

"Gibney, you gotta get me out of here."

"I give you my word that if they convict you, I'll get you out one night before the hanging."

"Yeah? What if they don't wait?"

"They'll have to wait, because I'll appeal."

"You're the educated one of us," Rickles said. "I'll trust you. But so help me, if I get up next to that noose and no one's stoppin' 'em, I'll spill my guts about you and Dodge."

"Keep your head, will you? It'll be all right, one way or the other. And I've got some money to give you."

The editor's throat was dry. He was mighty glad that Rickles didn't know the take in Dodge had been over twenty thousand. During the escape in the night, Gibney had managed to hide most of the cash in his own saddlebags, reducing the weight of the two money sacks. Before dawn, he had tossed a bag of money at Rickles, and they had parted. He didn't know until later how well he had divided the loot.

Back at the hotel, Hank paced his room, still shaken by Melanie's death. Nursing his sore left shoulder and dropping back on the bed with his six-gun still in his hand, he stared at the ceiling in the soft light of the lamp. Then he closed his tearful eyes and slept.

In the morning, when Hank went down to the hotel dining room for breakfast, he found himself sharing a table with Carter, Rosalee, and Gibney. They were dressed for church, already discussing the funeral that would follow the services. Rosalee's eyes were red from crying.

"So you got shot at again," Gibney said to Hank. "I guess I don't need anyone but you for the latest news. And I'm told I'll be acting as the defense lawyer. You must know you don't have a case for murder."

"I don't know that," Hank said.

Rosalee shook her head sadly. "Poor Melanie."

Her father reached over to take her hand in his.

"But you were lookin' for Harrington's murderer," Gibney reminded Hank. "You seem to have forgotten that."

"No, I haven't. I'm still looking for France, the man Harrington was after. France is supposed to be fifty or so and gray-haired."

Carter frowned. "Like me?"

"Like you and a few others." Hank avoided Rosalee's unhappy gaze. "What do you know about Sloan?"

"Good man," Carter said. "Runs his cattle, takes care of his men. Keeps his nose clean. Loved his daughter."

"And Tanner?"

Carter made a face. "That slimy gambler? The less I know about him and his hired guns, the better."

"What about Smite?" Hank asked.

"The sheriff does half a job," Carter said. "Most

he ever does is lock up a drunk. I figure he's gettin' a little under the table from 'most everyone. But I don't think he has guts enough for a killing."

"Well, they're not the only ones who could be France," Gibney said. "This town is loaded with shady characters."

"What about you?" Hank asked.

"I told you, Marshal," the editor said, "I'm clean as a whistle. Educated men don't have to rob or murder."

Hank set down his cup and stood up. "We'll set the trial for this afternoon."

"What's the hurry?" Gibney asked.

"Folks might not get through the night without wanting to hang him."

"You said a mouthful," Carter agreed. "Melanie was liked by everyone in this town. I figure Sloan's doing a slow burn about now. When he pulls himself together, there's no telling what will happen. Be more than vigilantes this time. It would be a mob."

Hank tipped his hat to Rosalee, nodded to the men, and went outside in the crisp morning air. The sun was shining, but dark clouds were moving in from the west.

He knew how Sloan felt about losing Melanie to violence. He felt the same way about losing his cousin. Even now, his eyes stung with the memory of finding Harrington's body. He swallowed hard and moved along the boardwalk.

The street was busy for a Sunday morning. A

mule train—twenty mules, loaded with supplies—was standing in front of the general store. Wagons were in the street. Several couples in their Sunday best were moving up the hill for Sunday services and Melanie's funeral. Soon the Carters and Gibney joined the procession toward the church. There was no sign of Sloan.

At the sheriff's office, Hank walked in to find Smite stretched out on the bunk, sound asleep and snoring. Hank kicked the bunk, waking the man, who sat up disoriented and angry. "What the devil do you want, Marshal?"

"Get the mayor to set up the trial for three o'clock this afternoon. A good place would be that storehouse where they held the dance."

"Yeah, that'd work all right. Now can I go back to sleep?"

Hank nodded and went back outside, down to the river's edge, where he gazed at the busy white water. The sky was darkening, the sun no longer visible.

He walked down to the Silver Palace. Inside, he found Stumpy playing cards with two miners. Several men lounged at a far table. Sugar was behind the bar, alone. She smiled as he walked over to talk with her. Her bruises had been powdered over. She thanked him for his help at the dance, adding, "I'm glad you're still alive."

"Trial's at three o'clock. You have any idea who would have been payin' Rickles to back shoot me?"

"Half the town."

"Where's Tanner?"

She nodded toward his office. Hank walked over to the door and shoved it open. An annoyed Tanner looked up from behind his desk, his face twisted. "Don't you know how to knock, Marshal?"

"Too easy to get shot that way."

"I got no reason to gun you, and if I did, it'd be out in the street, fair and square. I know you Darringers have a reputation for being fast guns, but I'm not one bit afraid of you."

"Trial's at three o'clock."

"Why should I care?"

"You didn't pay Rickles to gun me?"

"No. Are you goin' around askin' that question? Who do you think will say yes? You're crazy, Marshal."

Hank was annoyed, knowing the man was right. Still, he had to ask the question. It might make for a more interesting trial.

Hank closed the door behind him as he left the office. He noticed that Stumpy was sitting alone now. As he shuffled cards, Stumpy nodded to him. Hank walked over but didn't sit down.

"I was gonna tell you it was Rickles tried to gun you, but you got him first," Stumpy said.

"You seen Yancy this morning?"

"No."

Before he could turn away, Hank heard a strange voice. "Marshal!"

Turning slowly, Hank looked across at the man

who had entered the swinging doors with gun in hand. It was the bug-eyed, smaller Smith brother. He looked wild. His jaw was wrapped tight with bandages. His gun hand was shaking. His voice was weird. "My big brother just died from that hole in his gut! You killed both of my brothers! And now I'm gonna kill you!"

Everyone scrambled to get out of the way, disappearing behind the bar and overturned tables. Hank stood still, waiting. Drawing against a pulled gun was a dead man's play.

"You're a fast gun," Smith snarled. "So this is how I'm gonna make it fair. Go ahead, draw."

Hank's hand rested near his holster. He was tired of killing. Yet this time, he could be the one who died. His throat was dry, and his heart was drumming.

"You scared, Marshal?"

Hank didn't move. He wanted the man to be nervous.

Impatient, Smith suddenly aimed and squeezed the trigger. As his shot went off, Hank drew and fired. Smith's bullet whistled by Hank's neck. Smith jumped backward, startled by the slug in his chest.

Grabbing himself, blood running through his fingers, his eyes wild, Smith tried to speak. Instead, he slowly collapsed into a sprawling heap on the floor, kicking once before he died.

Hank stood quiet and grim. Slowly he holstered

his gun. The bystanders came out of hiding. There were whispers about the Darringer fast draw.

Tanner came out of his office. Hank turned to meet his gaze. The saloon owner was attempting to appear surprised and uninterested in the dead man.

"Well, Marshal," Stumpy said, "you got all three of 'em."

Hank left the saloon, weary of the whole thing. Now he would never know if the Smiths had killed his cousin. He had written a report to Marshal Wilcox before breakfast and stopped to mail it at the little post office on the main street.

He walked on to the livery and saddled his black stallion. The animal was so happy, it danced around as he led it into the street. He needed to ride, to feel the wind in his face. He had to clear his thoughts. He had to forget about that lovely young woman who had died in her father's arms. He had to accept having killed yet another man.

He rode the stallion up into the hills overlooking the town and wooded knolls. He could see cattle grazing far below to the northeast. Wagons were coming up along the river. Riderless horses were coming down the trail from the mines.

The air was fresh and clean. The sky was threatening.

He pulled on his leather coat, which had been tied behind the saddle. As he rode, he could see the Carter mansion, set back in the hills. Riding back to the ravine, he reined up, remembering again how he had kissed Rosalee there.

The rope was still dangling from the big tree.

He kept riding until high noon, setting the eager, energy-charged stallion into a gallop now and then. Its black coat gleamed with sweat.

Now he was heading back toward the main trail that led up to the mines. It was then that he saw Yancy coming down, riding a buckskin and leading a sorrel. On the sorrel was the body of a man, slumped over and tied down.

Yancy reined up when he saw Hank approaching.

"Nice stallion you have there," Yancy called.

Hank rode up to him and stopped his mount. He studied the fierce-looking man in buckskin, whose long, straggly hair and small black eyes set in a square, hard face made him look dangerous.

"You've been working, I see," Hank commented.

"Hogan. Wanted for rustlin'."

"Had to kill him?"

"He tried to kill me when I cornered him. Have you found this France hombre?"

"No. You figure you know who he is?"

"Maybe, but there's a big reward."

"I saw the poster once," Hank said. "But Smite doesn't have any copies."

"Stumpy carries it around with him."

Suddenly furious at Stumpy, Hank turned his stallion and set it to a gallop as he headed down the trail and into town. He unsaddled at the livery and rubbed down his mount. Then he headed back down the street and over to the Silver Palace.

Stumpy was at the bar, flirting with Sugar. He turned and saw Hank's face. The little man swallowed hard and headed for the corner table. Hank followed, sat down opposite him, and leaned forward, saying, "All right, Stumpy. Let's have the poster on France."

"How'd you find out I got it? Oh, Yancy, huh? Well, it will cost you, Marshal."

"No, it won't, because I'll have you locked up for obstructing justice."

Stumpy stared at him a long moment, then made a face. "No need to be threatenin', Marshal. You're gonna need me." Reaching inside his shirt, Stumpy pulled out the poster and reluctantly surrendered it.

Hank unrolled it. There was no picture. Just text he recognized:

WANTED DEAD OR ALIVE

Two men who murdered a United States Deputy Marshal and express guard in Dodge City on August 14, 1874. One of the men may be about fifty years old and gray. His name could be France. The other man was thinner and wore a red vest. $20,800.00 was taken from the express shipment.

REWARD of $5000.00 for information leading to the arrest of either man.

Hank grimaced as he folded the poster and shoved it inside his coat. Stumpy was nervous as the lawman stood, but Hank spun on his heel and walked out of the saloon. It was raining softly now.

Moving back into the main street, he saw Yancy's buckskin and the sorrel in front of the jail. The body had been removed. Yancy was collecting some getting-away money. Hank didn't like the idea that Yancy was making plans.

Dodging the rain, Hank headed for the hotel and entered the plush lobby. He paused, brushing water from himself as he saw the Carters and Sloan seated in the waiting area with Gibney.

Hank glanced at Rosalee's welcoming smile. He noticed that Carter and Gibney looked unusually relaxed.

Sloan was a wreck of a man, looking white-faced and lifeless. The funeral must have been painful. Rosalee was sitting between her father and Gibney.

Gibney didn't like the warm look that passed from her to Hank, and he reached to take her hand in his as if claiming her. Rosalee smiled at the editor.

They could hear the rain and the wind now. The storm was getting worse and louder, pounding against the windows.

"Maybe you should stay in town another night," Rosalee suggested to Sloan.

"I have to get back to the spread," the rancher replied. "Right after the trial."

They all stood up as Sloan began to leave, his

large body bent and stumbling. Rosalee caught his arm and reached up to kiss his cheek. Abruptly, the rancher drew her into his arms, hugging her for a moment. Then he turned, tears in his eyes as he walked away from them, through the lobby and out into the rain.

Rosalee went to the doorway, gazing after him. Hank came to stand at her side. She looked up at him, her eyes brimming.

"I feel so sorry for him," she said.

Her fingers slid into Hank's, and the editor, annoyed, hurried to join them. Her hands fell back to her sides.

"Look, Marshal," Gibney said, suddenly angry, "you're wasting your time."

"Let's get one thing straight," Hank said directly to Gibney. "I plan to take her away from you."

Rosalee was stunned. Her father, who was back at the couch, couldn't hear the conversation.

"You're crazy," Gibney sputtered.

Hank didn't look at Rosalee as he spun about and went through the doors, out onto the porch. He couldn't believe what he had just said. Sure, he wanted to marry her, but he felt he'd been foolish to announce his intentions when the chances were she'd never accept his proposal.

Gibney could offer social position, a big house, and a comfortable life. A lawman could offer only a little house with a lot of loneliness, and maybe early widowhood. Any woman would choose Gibney over that.

He paused, staring at the darkness of the storm. He didn't have his slicker. The rain was coming down in torrents. He didn't want to return to his room while Rosalee and the others were still in the lobby.

Pulling down his hat, he darted into the rain, heading for the Eatery, where Hattie gave him a good meal and fussed over him. By then it was nearly two and the rain had stopped. He walked outside, breathing the fresh clean air and squinting in the bright sunlight.

A wagon was fighting its way through the mud to the livery. There were two horses in front of the jail across the street. Yancy's buckskin stood with its head down. The roan next to it had another body hung over the saddle and covered with a slicker.

Hank grimaced. He pulled his wide-brimmed hat down tight on his brow and fought his way through the mud. Entering the jail, he found Smite, half dressed, at his desk, with Yancy standing in front of it.

"Well, Marshal?" Smite grunted. "What do you want?"

"Who's on the saddle this time?" Hank demanded.

"Rustler, and wanted for murder," Yancy said, smiling his slimy smile. "Got him down at the smelter. Two in one day. Not bad, eh?"

"You had to bring him in dead?" Hank asked.

"He tried to kill me," Yancy claimed blandly.

"So did his friend, but his friend wasn't wanted, so I just left him out there. I figure they'll bury him."

"You're wearin' out your welcome," Hank said.

"I got my rights," Yancy told him.

Hank was frustrated. Yancy would just keep hauling in wanted men, shot dead and strung across the saddle, and Hank couldn't stop him. He was probably paying Stumpy for every wanted poster the little man had stashed away.

Hank walked outside. Tanner was coming from the hotel. Hank didn't like the man, and he followed him around the corner on the boardwalk, where they both stopped.

"Where are you from, Tanner?"

"I was born in New Orleans. Why?"

"You got family there?"

The saloon owner studied Hank a moment, then nodded. "Why do you want to know, Marshal?"

"Just tryin' to figure you out."

Tanner smiled. "I'm a gambler by trade. Married into money. She died in New Orleans, so I came West. Aim to make my fortune. And I plan to marry again. I've set my sights on Rosalee Carter. You take offense to that?"

"Yes, I do."

Tanner grinned. "You're not alone, but I know what I'm doing, Marshal. And don't be forgettin', I'm pretty fast with this six-gun, so don't get in my way."

Hank was steaming, but Tanner suddenly de-

cided it was time to set his plan in motion. He left
Hank and returned to the hotel to find Carter,
whom he brought to a quiet corner of the lobby
where no one could hear.

"All right, Tanner, what do you want?"

"Your daughter."

"What? You're loco."

"Listen to me, Carter. I know someone who was
well aware that Rosalee's mother was one-quarter
Cheyenne. He's up in Denver and will come anytime I say. I even know that Rosalee's grandmother
died at Sand Creek. Now, if word gets out around
here, you'll have to hide Rosalee. Folks ain't forgot
the Indian wars. Some lost family to the Cheyenne."

"You're crazy, Tanner."

"It's the truth and you know it. Now, I won't
say one word to anyone, and I won't bring Loney
from Denver, but I want Rosalee."

"Loney? Ha! He's been dead since last year."

"You're bluffing, Carter."

"Go ahead, write him a letter. See if you get an
answer. And what's more, he'd only be guessin',
just like you."

"I'll call your bluff, Carter. I'll even sell out the
saloon and dance hall. I'd like to be a gentleman
again. And I have some education, as you know.
She'd still be a lady."

Carter's face was red with anger, but he was
careful. "Tanner, you sell out your saloon and

dance hall, and you show me you're a gentleman, and I'll think about it."

"That's a start, but we both know how it will end up. Rosalee's going to be my wife."

"You know Gibney plans to marry her."

"I can take care of him."

"Seems to me your mother was French, Tanner. Maybe they called you Frenchy. Maybe you're that France feller. I could set Darringer on you mighty easy."

"I'd still get the word out about your daughter. You can't win, Carter."

Carter wasn't sure what to do about this man, but he didn't want him shouting in town about Rosalee's heritage.

By the time Tanner left, Carter was gritting his teeth. He took a deep, angry breath and went out into the bright sunlight. He stood on the porch, his mind reeling. The only solution was to be rid of Tanner, once and for all.

One thing Carter was certain of, Tanner was wanted somewhere for something. A man like that, in his business, had to have been in trouble. The gambler would never submit to arrest. In fact, the man would be furious at the thought, even pull his gun. That could end it.

He beckoned Hank, who was walking down the street. The two met in front of the hotel, with no one in earshot.

"Marshal, I've been thinkin' about this feller France you're after. You know, Tanner's mother was French. Seems to me they used to call him Frenchy."

Hank listened, trying to read behind the man's words. Something had made Carter so angry that his face was red and quivering.

"You tyin' a knot in my tail?" Hank asked.

"You go ask Tanner, but don't let him know I said it."

"He's after Rosalee, is he?"

"You guessed it, but I'm givin' you the truth, Marshal. Three years ago he and Sloan came to town together with a lot of loot. I know they'd come from Dodge. They coulda killed that marshal. And the day Harrington was killed? I heard the shot when I was ridin' down by the river. Then I saw Tanner riding in from that direction."

"You willin' to testify?"

"Well, sure."

"But you're hopin' it won't come to that."

"You got me wrong, Marshal."

"All right, but you'll have to come to the jail and sign a complaint."

Carter reluctantly nodded and followed him over to the empty jailhouse. In a shaky hand, Carter wrote down his accusations, sweat trickling down his face. When he was done, he left silently and Hank pocketed the paper. He stood grim, watching Carter cross back over to the hotel.

Hank was on the spot. A citizen had given him a lead, signed a complaint, and was prepared to testify. He had to arrest Tanner, even if it ended up in a fight. And his every instinct told him Tanner would resist arrest.

But if the gambler was the man who killed Harrington, it would finally put Hank's misery and desire for vengeance to rest. Maybe then he could grieve for the man who had been like a father to him. Uneasy, he checked and reloaded his six-gun.

He turned and walked back through the mud to the other side of the street, then down the boardwalk toward the saloons that lined the river.

Chapter Seven

*I*n front of the Silver Palace, Tanner was talking
to Stumpy. The saloon owner sensed something
was wrong as he turned to watch Hank approach.
"All right, Marshal, what's on your mind?"

"I've just been told you used to be called
Frenchy."

"So what?"

"And I understand you and Sloan came here together three years ago, with a lot of money."

"We got here the same time, that's all."

"I'm told you came directly from Dodge City.
And that you were riding along the river about the
time Harrington was killed."

"You're plumb loco, Marshal."

"I have a witness."

"That's not enough, and you know it."

"A jury has to decide that," Hank said.

"You're not arrestin' me, Marshal."

Stumpy suddenly hobbled inside the saloon.
Faces were pressed to the dirty windows. Hank saw
Sugar in the doorway, backing away.

120

Tanner stepped out into the mud. He was well dressed in a dark suit, his fancy boots sinking in the slush. He pushed his coat back behind his six-gun. Confident, swaggering, he was certain he was going to best a Darringer. It would make everyone clear a wide path for him. The thought was pleasing.

Hank stepped into the street. It was cold and breezy. He could hear the roar of the river to his right. It was not a good morning to die. Not here in the wet mud.

From the corner of his eye, Hank saw Yancy standing behind the swinging doors with Stumpy. Other faces were crowded at the windows. He wondered if Sugar would weep for him.

Tanner was menacing, his dark eyes narrowed.

"Marshal," Gibney called from behind Hank, "I—"

Hank didn't turn, his gaze fixed on Tanner.

Abruptly, Gibney hurried past them and into the saloon.

Tanner was smiling that same slimy sneer. Holding his head high, he appeared confident and proud. With his slim left hand, he pushed his small-brimmed hat back from his brow.

The sun was rising behind Tanner. Hank's hat was pulled down, barely shielding his eyes. Sweat was running down the lawman's back.

"You call it, Marshal," the gambler said.

"You're under arrest, Tanner."

"Not a chance."

And Tanner's right hand slid to his six-gun.

Tanner made his move, swift and sure, whipping up his six-gun and firing, but Hank had already drawn and shot him dead in the chest. The lawman's draw had been so swift no one had seen his hand move. It was over in a split second.

Tanner gasped, staggering backward with the impact.

Hank slowly lowered his six-gun, watching as the gambler tried to fire again. The man's first shot had whistled by Hank's ear. The second roared uselessly into the mud.

Tanner dropped to his knees, staring at Hank, who came slowly forward. "It wasn't me," the gambler gasped in a barely audible voice.

Hank was shattered as the man collapsed into the mud. Had he just shot an innocent man?

Stumpy and the others came out of the saloon.

"So you found out about it," Stumpy said. "I was goin' to tell you, Marshal. He robbed that bank down in Austin, that's for sure."

"You had him pegged for the Dodge killing?"

"No, Marshal, I wasn't real sure about that. Besides, I was gonna tell you about Austin, as soon as I was sure."

"Are you sure now?" Hank demanded.

Stumpy reached inside his shirt and pulled out another poster. "Yeah, I, uh, just found this."

Hank jerked the poster out of the little man's hands, figuring Stumpy had been taking bribes from Tanner to keep silent. He unfolded the poster. There was no picture, but the descriptions were plenty clear:

> *WANTED DEAD OR ALIVE*
> *Frenchy Tanner and an unidentified companion for robbery of the Austin Citizens' Bank on October 15, 1874, and murder of two men. Frenchy Tanner is a tall, thin man with black hair and a mustache. His companion is described as red-faced with a jutting chin.*

Hank thought of Harris Sloan, who would fit the second description. He tried to visualize Tanner and the rancher robbing the Texas bank, coming to town, and splitting their loot. It didn't figure. Sloan just didn't seem that kind of man.

"You need any more help, Marshal, let me know," Stumpy offered.

"You mean now that your meal ticket is dead?" Hank grunted.

Tanner was still lying in the mud. The shots had brought the doctor and Smite, who noticed that Tanner's six-gun was still in his right hand.

Hank felt drained. He turned and looked at Sugar, who was waving from the window. Gibney came out of the saloon and knelt with the doctor.

Yancy walked slowly into the sunlight. He looked mean as sin, his scraggly black hair blowing about his thick neck. His small black eyes were gleaming. "Not bad, Marshal," he said.

"Not bad?" Stumpy sounded indignant. "You're loco, Yancy. That's the fastest draw you'll ever see, anywhere."

Gibney stood up, shaking his head. "He's dead, all right. What was it about, Marshal?"

Hank shrugged. "I was arrestin' him for the Dodge killin', but before he died, he said it wasn't him. You gotta believe a man who's dyin'."

"But he was wanted for the bank robbery in Austin," Stumpy argued. "And murder, right, Marshal?"

"Yes."

Gibney asked to see the poster, then returned it.

"You're sure giving me a lot to write about," the editor said. "In fact, I may just settle down to write a book about you."

"Forget it," Hank said, dragging his boots out of the mud. As he turned to go up the street, he saw Carter. The man had been watching before going back around the jail and crossing to the hotel.

Hank wanted to be angry at Carter, but Tanner had still been guilty of something. He guessed that Tanner was after Rosalee and her father had done whatever he could to stop it. As he walked back up the boardwalk, Gibney tried to keep pace.

"What are you so mad about, Marshal?" the editor asked.

"The people in this town."

"Well, you already found out that Rickles tried to shoot you. I doubt you'll ever find out who killed

Harrington. For all you know, that France fellow isn't even here. If I were you, I'd just ride out."

"And leave you with Rosalee?"

"Come on, Marshal! You just killed another man. You got the Smiths and Tanner, and someday somebody's going to kill you. What kind of life would you offer her?"

Hank crossed over to the hotel to speak to Carter, who was waiting for him on the porch. Gibney went on his way up the street.

Hank climbed the steps to face Carter. There was no one else within earshot. The two men studied each other.

"You set Tanner up," Hank said.

"You going to arrest me?"

"No. He was wanted for robbery and murder in Texas."

Carter drew a long deep breath, then leaned on a post. "Marshal, if I was you, I'd just ride on out, right after the trial."

"I'm gettin' tired of hearin' that."

"You're wearin' out your welcome."

"I'm wondering if Stumpy has any more posters. He seems to have been collecting them. I'm surprised he's still alive, but I reckon he comes cheap. Maybe you've been payin' him a little to keep quiet."

"You're wrong, Marshal."

It was then that Rosalee came out of the hotel. She was dressed in green velvet and looked as beautiful as ever. Her long, shining black hair was lifting in the breeze. Her face was flushed. "Father, I heard gunshots."

"The Marshal here just shot Tanner."

She was surprised. "But why? Was he the man you were looking for?"

Hank shrugged. "He was wanted in Texas for robbery and murder. He drew on me."

"You have a dirty job, Marshal," Carter observed. "You live by the gun. Someday you'll be cut down in the street, just like Tanner. And if you stick around here, it may be sooner than you think."

Rosalee was distressed. "Father, don't say such things."

"It's all right, honey," Carter said. "And listen, you don't have to go to the trial."

"But I want to," she protested.

"And she's my only witness," Hank added.

Carter shrugged. "I'll get your cape."

Her father went back inside, and she turned to Hank. "Father was so angry at you. Why?"

"He figures I'm after you."

"But you must know about me and Nelson."

He hesitated, pushing his hat back from his brow. She stared at him. He knew then that she would do whatever her father said. Heartsick, he turned away.

Still shaken by the shooting, Hank walked up the street. He had faced Tanner for something the man had not done. It didn't matter that Tanner was guilty of something else. He could have killed an innocent man.

When Harrington was alive, coaching him, it had all seemed so right. He had virtually worshiped his cousin and had hung on his every word. He had copied Harrington's life. Now everything was going wrong.

He saw Gibney and Sloan in front of the newspaper office. As he walked toward them, Gibney disappeared inside. The big rancher turned to face Hank.

They nodded to each other and began to walk together. Up ahead, a crowd was moving toward the storehouse. In a little while, Melanie's killer would be on trial. Sloan was colorless and looked a century old.

"I just heard about Tanner," Sloan said quietly.

"You fit the poster," Hank noted.

No defenses left, Sloan nodded, his voice low. "Arrest me if you want, but I didn't kill anyone in Austin. I didn't even rob the bank."

They paused on the boardwalk as Sloan continued, "Tanner and I were comin' here from New Orleans. He left me with the horses while he went into the bank with a friend. Said they'd be only a minute. Next thing I know, there was shootin', and Tanner came charging out with a couple of sacks. His friend was shot down inside."

Sloan looked around to make sure no one could hear. "I rode off with him, sure," the rancher said. "Everyone was shootin' at him and me too. What was I supposed to do? He gave me some of the money. I took it because I figured we'd be on the run and I'd need it. But when we got here, the whole town was full of men like us. Tanner, he went and bought the saloon. All I wanted was to get back to ranchin' and have my daughter join me." He cleared his throat. "I've never done a wrong thing in my life, Marshal, except to take some of that money. If you arrest me for that, I'll hang for sure."

Hank's mind churned. He believed this man. He didn't want the rancher to hang, but that was what would happen. Yet somehow this man had to right his wrong. He wondered how his cousin would have handled it. Slowly the answer came.

"How much money did Tanner give you?" Hank asked.

"Nine hundred dollars. When I put that together with what I had from a place I had sold in Louisiana, it was enough to get a ranch goin'."

"You got nine hundred dollars now?"

"Well, sure, but—"

"You get me a bank draft payable to the Citizens' Bank, and I'll send it to Austin. No need for your name to be on it."

Sloan couldn't believe his ears. He was astounded. "But why?" the rancher asked.

"Chances are, no witnesses could peg you in Austin. It'd be a waste of my time to haul you in. That description on the poster could be any one of a hundred men."

"But I still don't—"

"Let's say it's for Melanie."

Sloan's face was ashen. "For Melanie," he murmured.

They continued walking. It was almost three o'clock and time for Rickles' trial. Almost everyone else was off the street and waiting at the storehouse.

Sloan cleared his throat. "There's somethin' I got to tell you, Marshal. You've been fair with me. When I heard you was comin' to Prospect, I sent for Yancy. Not to gun you in the back. He was to pick a fair fight and get you off our hands."

"I figured someone had sent for him."

"He wanted a thousand from me and Tanner to get you."

They paused again, their eyes meeting with understanding. Hank liked this man. Slowly he grinned. "Worth a thousand, am I?"

"It's worse than that," Sloan said. "Yancy's gone crazy since he saw Carter's daughter. Right away, he starts tellin' us he wants five hundred and Rosalee. Tanner and me, we both told him it was no deal."

"You figure he's going to go after her?"

"No doubt about it."

Hank's face was dark with fury. Yancy, the bounty hunter, the fast gun, the killer of men, had his evil mind set on the beautiful Rosalee. The very thought was like a knife in Hank's gut. "You'd better warn Carter," he said.

"I plan to."

They left the street and walked to the storehouse. Inside, they found most of the town crowded into rows of chairs on each side of a center aisle. Up front were tables. A desk had been hauled in for the judge.

Hank could see mixed feelings in the faces of the rough miners and merchants. Not one of them seemed too happy about his presence. They probably hadn't wept for Harrington. In fact, there was downright disapproval of the law's interfering in their affairs. But they had liked Melanie.

The Carters and Gibney were entering now. Rosalee's eyes were still red from weeping. She sat with her father in the back row. Gibney came to the front of the room, where Hank was standing.

Gibney was in turmoil. He had found a decent life again; he planned to marry Rosalee and have access to her father's money. That indiscretion in Dodge City had been a freak turn in his life. Rickles had been bad company, leading him into trouble at a time when Gibney couldn't find work worthy of his education. France had become the editor's criminal identity. Gibney had been forced to kill the guard and lawman when they turned on him. It had been dark, and escape had been easy. Rickles couldn't react quickly enough and had been little help.

So far, Rickles had not used what happened in Dodge City against Gibney, and the editor felt some guilt about not having freed him. Still, Gibney was convinced he could secure a verdict of not guilty.

Winslow, the short, stout, mean-faced mayor and judge of the town, looked the situation over as he sat behind his desk. No one had stood when he had entered to take his place at the bench. That put him in a bad humor. "Where's the prisoner?" he demanded.

They all turned to watch as Smite and Rickles, his hands cuffed in front of him, entered from the back door. As they came forward, Sloan entered and sat beside Carter in the back row.

The sheriff and the prisoner were seated at a table facing the judge on the left. Gibney joined them. Hank walked to the table on the right and stood with his back to the crowd. He removed his leather coat and glanced down at the shiny badge on his vest.

As acting prosecutor, Hank was going farther than his cousin would have liked. Yet he had to go through with it.

"Now, let me tell you right off," Judge Winslow said, "that I was a lawyer for twenty years in Philadelphia. I realize we are holding trial under primitive conditions, but I will not allow any disturbance in this courtroom."

The crowd, mumbling among themselves, slowly quieted.

"What are the charges?" the judge asked.

"Attempted murder of a Federal marshal," Hank said, "and the murder of Melanie Sloan."

Hank considered the judge for a long moment. The man looked mean as sin, but there was something solid about him that made Hank believe he would be fair.

Rickles got to his feet and pleaded not guilty. The short, wiry man was grim, his beady brown eyes fixed on the judge. At his side, Gibney rose also. When they sat down, Gibney whispered his reassurance that if they lost at this trial, he would get Rickles out of jail tonight.

A jury of twelve men was picked and seated to Hank's right. They looked serious but uncertain, having to give a fair trial to the man responsible for Melanie's death.

The barber was Hank's first witness. Small and white-faced, he was nervous but said he'd seen Rickles nodding to whatever the lawman had said. But Hank discovered the usually talkative man was hard of hearing, forcing Hank to speak loudly.

Gibney pounced on that opportunity during his cross-examination, speaking low.

"What did you say?" the barber asked, bending forward.

"I asked what you heard the marshal say," Gibney said softly.

"Your Honor," Hank said, "Mr. Gibney is deliberately speaking so low no one could hear."

"All right then," Gibney said in a normal voice, "what did you hear Mr. Rickles say?"

"What did you say?" the barber asked.

The crowd broke into laughter, and Winslow

hammered his gavel. It took awhile for the room to settle down, but by then, Hank knew he had lost this witness. The barber said he didn't hear any words that he could understand. He only saw Rickles nodding his head.

Smite was called. The sheriff let it be known from his first answers that he wasn't going to remember anything. It was obvious he knew the best way to keep his job was to stay alive. He claimed he heard nothing and saw nothing.

"Sheriff, you were standing right there when I turned Mr. Rickles over and started to question him," Hank reminded him.

"Well, I was busy lookin' for whoever shot him."

Everyone laughed again, because they knew Hank was the gunman.

Frowning, Winslow hammered on the desk once more.

Since the sheriff was noncommittal, Gibney did not bother to cross-examine him.

The doctor, who had been called out on an emergency, entered the courtroom. He had not heard either witness and wondered why everyone seemed in such good humor. Hank called him to the stand.

"Doctor, last night after the dance, shots were fired. Did you hear them?" Hank asked.

"Yes, sure. I had been out late delivering Mrs. Robinson's ninth child. I was up in my office and just turned out the light."

"Then what happened?"

"Well, sir, I heard the shooting and went outside

on the landing. I saw you running across the street from the hotel and into the alley. So I went to the back to look down, and I saw you chasing someone up behind the express office. He was shooting at you, so you shot him."

"And then?"

"I could see whoever you shot was down for good, so I went back down the stairs and over to where you were. I took my bag, just in case he was alive."

"And who had I shot?"

"Mr. Rickles there."

"Was he hurt bad?"

"He thought he was," the doctor said. "In fact, he was convinced he was dying."

"Objection!" Gibney shouted. "The witness is not a mind reader."

"Sustained," the judge said. "The jury will disregard."

"What happened next?" Hank asked the doctor.

"You asked him if he had shot you several times. He just nodded his head."

"Objection," Gibney called. "Mr. Rickles was hurt bad. Instead of nodding his head, he may have just been gasping in pain."

"Your Honor," Hank said, "if we could continue, we'll clear that up."

"Proceed," Winslow said.

"Doctor, what other questions did I ask Mr. Rickles and what were his responses?"

"Well, Marshal, you asked him who paid or

helped him, but he couldn't answer as I was working on him. Then you asked him if he had killed Harrington, and he shook his head."

"So in answer to the first few questions," Hank said, "he nodded his answers, but to the last, he shook his head?"

"Yes, that's right."

"Were these deliberate movements?"

"Yes, they were."

"Your Honor," said Hank, "since by shaking his head Mr. Rickles was making just as deliberate a movement as he was by nodding it, I submit that he understood and was answering the questions."

The judge then overruled Gibney's prior objection, and Hank continued. "Doctor, what happened next?"

"Mr. Rickles asked me if he was going to die. I said he was not."

"So do you believe, prior to that moment, that he really thought he was going to die?"

"Yes."

"Your Honor," Gibney protested, "this is all hearsay."

"If Mr. Rickles believed he was going to die, then the nod of his head would be a dying declaration," the judge said. "The testimony will also be allowed as an admission of guilt. Overruled."

"What happened next?" Hank asked the doctor.

The medic testified that he was called to Melanie's room and that she was dying from a bullet wound when he examined her. He told of the broken window.

Gibney's cross-examination was brief and stumbling.

Hank was then forced to call Rosalee, who timidly walked up the aisle with everyone staring at her. She sat in a chair next to the judge's desk and swore to tell the truth. Nervous, she twined the ends of her hair around her fingers.

"Now, Miss Carter," Hank said, trying to be gentle as he saw the stress in her pretty face, "last night after the dance, what happened after you went to your room at the hotel?"

She moistened her lips and told how she couldn't sleep, how he had joined her on the veranda, and how they had talked at least ten minutes. She said they were standing near a window, Hank outlined by the light.

"Then what happened?" he asked.

"Someone shot at you. You threw me aside and jumped from the veranda. The bullet went through the window behind us. I thought I heard someone cry out, but I wasn't sure. I was afraid it was me."

"And then?" Hank prompted.

She stared at him and moistened her lips again. Painfully she told of finding Melanie.

When Hank had finished asking questions, Gibney stood up. He gazed a long moment at the woman he loved. There was very little he could do. He knew she would not change her testimony. Her tears were tough to face.

"No questions," he said, ignoring Rickles' angry stare. Rosalee was allowed to return to her seat in the back row.

Still, Gibney seemed unshaken as he stood up.

"Your Honor," the editor said, "the facts are clear. My client admits he shot at the marshal just to scare him and make him leave town. That's not an attempt to murder. Just a red-blooded young man making it known he wanted to be left alone."

Gibney noted the jury's obvious agreement before continuing. "Mr. Rickles did not intend to kill Melanie Sloan. I can't believe any man in this courtroom would hold my client guilty of murder when he wasn't even aware of Miss Sloan's presence. I ask them to put themselves in his place. He feels terrible remorse. He had no intent to kill her."

As he rambled on, Gibney saw heads nod in the jury. They sympathized with Rickles. They, too, would have felt plenty rotten after that accident. And some of them may have had secret pasts and were not too happy about Federal law being in town. Any one of them, Gibney suggested, might have fired a shot at the lawman to frighten him out of town, if they had been brave enough.

When Gibney finished, the judge spoke gruffly. "Well, you made your arguments out of order, but we have to make do. Marshal?"

Hank stood up, the memory of Melanie's death still fresh in his mind. He squared his shoulders and looked at Rickles. Gibney was sitting straight in his chair, defying Hank to prove his client had tried to kill Melanie. Hank spoke clearly. "Your Honor, I figure if you shoot at one person with the intent to kill, and you miss, hitting a second person, then your intent to kill the first person is applied to the second."

"Your Honor!" Gibney protested. "That's outrageous!"

"But it's the law," the judge informed him.

"Your Honor," Hank said, "it also seems like firing a rifle at anybody has got to be intent to kill. And anyone who fires at a hotel window has got to know he can hit someone inside."

The judge nodded. Then the white-faced Gibney stared as the judge instructed the jury to accept Hank's definitions of murder and attempted murder.

The jury didn't retire, mumbling among themselves instead. Abruptly, a burly miner stood up, looking important. In a squeaky voice he announced, "Your Honor, we find Rickles guilty on both counts. We say we oughta go hang 'im afore sundown."

The judge banged his gavel and asked Rickles to stand. His body shaking from his wobbly knees to his chin, Rickles had to lean on the table for support.

"Have you anything to say before I pass sentence?" the judge asked the prisoner, who couldn't answer.

"Your Honor," Gibney said quickly, "we are going to appeal."

"So noted," the judge said, "but for purposes of this trial, Mr. Rickles is sentenced to life in prison at Canon City. The sheriff will resume custody. Court dismissed."

Rickles looked as if he had a mouthful of angry words. Gibney quickly took his arm and spun him around. They walked out ahead of the bored Smite. At times, the editor pushed Rickles to walk faster.

Outside, it was nearly dark. Rickles was snarling.

"Blast you, Gibney! If you don't—"

"Calm down. We'll talk later. And don't worry."

It was windy and cold, the darkness closing in on them as they walked. Gibney glanced back at Smite, who was taking his time.

"Just wait," Gibney murmured. "I'll get you out tonight. And I'll have a thousand dollars for you."

Gibney promised at the very least to slip him a pistol through the jail window while Smite was sleeping.

All the while, Gibney was trying to figure a way to silence this man forever. He resented this need. He had made a good life here. Somehow he had to close the door on this disruption.

Back inside the courtroom, people were getting to their feet, not certain how to react. They filed out into the darkness, talking among themselves about the first real trial they had had. No one wanted Rickles to escape a hanging. Yet they were not stirred up enough just now to arrange a lynching. They had too much to think about and were in no hurry.

Sloan, a shattered man, left with the crowd.

Hank was standing near the table as the judge came around to talk to him. Short, stout, and mean, the judge accosted Hank as the lawman pulled on his leather coat. "I'm sorry I didn't get to know this Marshal Harrington. You find out who killed him?"

Hank shook his head, and the judge turned away. Hank noticed that the Carters were still at the back of the now nearly empty room. He walked over to them. Rosalee had regained her color.

"We're going home now," Carter said.

"You did well," Rosalee told Hank, managing a smile.

Carter took her arm and led her out into the night. Hank watched, weary, worn to the bone.

He walked down to the Eatery, where he sat quietly with his back to the wall. Everyone in the busy room buzzed about the trial. Hattie came and chatted with him briefly. He was exhausted and soon headed for the hotel.

In his room at last, he stretched out, still fully clothed and wearing his leather coat, staring at the dirty ceiling. He still didn't know who killed Harrington. Maybe the murderer was the man called France, the criminal Harrington had been hunting. But who was France, and who was his accomplice?

*   *   *

While Hank was hammering out his thoughts, Gibney was marking time until the early hours of the morning. He could wait no longer, because Rickles might start shooting off his mouth.

As he expected, the jailhouse door was unlocked. Smite was a careless man who was so indifferent to lawbreakers that no one had a grudge against him. He always felt safe.

Gibney slowly opened the door. On his left in the dim light of the lamp, he saw Smite snoring peacefully. The sheriff's holstered gun was hanging on the hat rack. Rickles' gun was still on the desk.

After closing the door behind him while Rickles watched, Gibney carefully shoved the window shutters aside. He then opened the window all the way up and blocked it.

He went to the desk, found the keys, and quietly handed them to Rickles. While the prisoner quickly freed himself, the editor took Smite's gun from its holster. As Rickles came out of the cell, Gibney turned and shot him square between the eyes with Smite's gun.

Rickles stared at him even as he collapsed and died.

Before Rickles hit the floor, Gibney caught up the dead man's gun from the desk.

Still snorting from sleep, Smite leaped up from his bunk. The editor turned and fired Rickles' gun directly into the sheriff's chest. The big man gasped and fell back, dead. Gibney knelt and put the sheriff's gun in his fist. Then he closed Rickles' hand over his own weapon.

Gibney reached for the windowsill, climbed out, and charged out into the alley, running behind the buildings.

Up in his hotel room, Hank jumped out of his bed. Still fully dressed and half asleep, he grabbed his six-gun. The first shot had nagged him from sleep. Now the second brought him wide-awake.

Chapter Eight

*H*ank had leaped from his bed, nearly knocking over the oil lamp, when gunfire echoed in the predawn hour. Now he ran from his room and took the stairs several steps at a time. He rushed through the empty lobby and out onto the porch.

The jailhouse door was open, pale light spilling forth. Half-dressed men were coming down the street. Hank charged down the steps, six-gun in hand, and rushed across to beat the crowd. He sprang to the open doorway, his weapon ready.

Just inside, his gun in hand, Smite lay on his back on the floor. Blood had spilled from his chest. His eyes were open, staring at the ceiling.

The cell door was open. Lying on his back in front of it was Rickles, gun in hand. He had been shot between the eyes. His gaze was fixed on the ceiling as well.

"My gosh!" Gibney exclaimed behind Hank.

Others crowded up close. "Looks like a jail-break," one of the men said. "How did he get a gun?"

"Someone must have slipped it to him," another man said.

Hank checked the bodies. Both men were dead. He surveyed the scene. It looked like a jailbreak, all right. Too much like one. The jail keys were dangling from the open cell door. The window near the bunk was open to the alley.

Hank stood aside as the doctor entered. Then he walked back into the fading darkness.

Men with lanterns were running all over the alley, obliterating any possible clues. Hank could only shake his head. Still half-dressed, Gibney was on his heels. It was nearly light now.

"What do you think happened?" the editor asked as he shoved his shirt into his pants.

"I don't know."

"Looks like someone slipped Rickles a gun, doesn't it? Then Rickles got the sheriff to open up, and Smite went for a gun, trying to stop him. Yes, that has to be it."

"That what you're planning to write?"

"Well, doesn't it make sense?"

Hank paused, turning to look at the editor. First light was falling on Gibney's blond hair and handsome face. This man was full of answers.

"I'm not sure Smite cared enough to get himself shot," Hank said.

While Hank and Gibney talked about the double killing, Rosalee Carter was awake in her room at the mansion. From her window she could see the sprinkle of lights in the town. It was nearly day-light, the early glow touching the shimmering leaves of the aspens near the house. She had an urge to saddle her mare and ride back to town. She was worried about Hank and wanted to see him.

After drawing on her riding clothes, she walked toward her door. A strange feeling was coming over her. Something was terribly wrong. Cold chills suddenly engulfed her. She wasn't sure why—until she opened the door.

Yancy was standing there, that eerie smile on his lips.

A silent scream welled up inside her as he seized her right arm. He held a big knife in his other hand, and he waved it at her throat. She was so terrified that no sound came from her. She fought his steel grip as he dragged her along with him to the back veranda door and down the rear, outside stairs.

Even in her panic she knew that if she struggled or screamed, her father would come and then Yancy would kill them both.

Hank stood on the boardwalk and watched the bodies being carried away. The crowd was milling about.

"Smite wasn't good for much," a man was saying.

"Neither was Rickles," another added.

"Whoever helped Rickles got plumb clean away," the first remarked.

Gibney was still there, acting important, gathering the facts for his paper.

Seeing the lights on in the Eatery, Hank cut across the street. Gibney followed. Inside, they sat together, Hank, as usual, with his back to the wall. A sleepy Hattie brought them coffee and breakfast. Hank could barely eat after what he had seen in the jail, but Gibney wolfed his meal.

"If it weren't for Rosalee," Gibney said, "I'd move to Denver. There'll never be any real law in this town. No offense, Marshal, but you have a whole state to cover."

Stumpy Potts came hobbling over. He looked happy. "Marshal, I think it was plenty good that Rickles got killed," the little man said. "I heard talk they was gonna lynch him this mornin', anyhow."

"You're interrupting my breakfast," Hank grunted.

"Now, that's no way to talk to a citizen," Stumpy protested. "I mean, I got my rights."

Hank glared at him. "You've been exercising a lot of rights, including extortion. If I ever hear of you holding a Wanted poster over a man's head just to get a few dollars out of him, I'll run you in and see that you're locked up for ten years."

"You didn't have to make a speech," Stumpy complained, making a face and turning away.

"I'm surprised he's still alive." Hank shook his head. "But I suppose he was always promisin' to keep a watch for more posters. And I reckon he was too smart to be greedy."

After breakfast, Hank and the editor went outside. The sun was rising in the eastern sky. Hank drew his leather coat tighter about him. There was a slight breeze. It was still cold. The street was nearly empty.

Far down the street, near the freighter's, he could see a mule train being loaded with more rails. And coming down the main trail, a man rode bareback on a sorrel horse, clinging to the mane.

Hank started walking toward him, Gibney following. As they neared, the editor suddenly spoke. "It's Tom, the Carters' handyman."

They broke into a run, reaching the nervous animal as the wounded man fell to the ground and rolled into the mud. His face was cut and bleeding, and blood was caked on his shirt. His white hair was streaked with blood.

Hank knelt and seized his hand. "What happened?"

"Get up there, Marshal!" the man gasped. "That Yancy . . . he got me and Mr. Carter. I think he was after Rosalee."

"Did you see her?" Hank asked, frantic.

"No. When I came to, I found Mr. Carter in his den, all sliced up like me. I couldn't get up the stairs, but when I called out, she didn't answer."

"Get him to the doctor," Hank said, rising.

Gibney shook his head. "I'm going with you."

Hank beckoned to a merchant who was opening

his store and asked him to help Tom. Then he ran toward the jail, Gibney on his heels. They took Winchester repeaters and shells, then hurried up the street again.

At the livery, they saddled and mounted. They rode out into the street and up the mountain trail. Hank's stallion soon left Gibney's bay far behind on the steep grade.

At the Carter home, Hank sprang from the saddle. Leaving his stallion at the railing, he charged into the house. He found two frightened elderly women servants huddling near the hearth. They pointed to a side room where there was a desk and a wall of books.

In the den, he found Carter, still alive, lying on the floor. Clumsily bandaged by the women, the man had been cut at the throat and chest. How he had survived this long, Hank didn't know, except that the man wanted his daughter to be saved and so had desperately fought to stay alive until help arrived.

Hank knelt. "Carter, it's me, Hank Darringer."

"Marshal," Carter moaned, staring up with glassy eyes, "Yancy has Rosalee. Please find her."

"I will," Hank promised.

As Hank started to rise, the man gripped his arm and rasped out, "Marshal, I didn't kill Harrington."

"Do you know who did?"

"No, but I wasn't at Dodge, either."

"All right," Hank said gently.

"All I ever done was kill a man over cards."

"Carter your real name?"

"No, but don't tell Rosalee."

"I won't."

Carter's bloody hand gripped Hank's arm more tightly. The man was not going to live much longer. The two women servants came into the den. One knelt to put her hand on the dying man's feverish brow.

Out of breath, Gibney came hurrying into the room.

Hank freed his arm and stood up. "Stay with him."

"I'm goin' with you," Gibney declared. "I don't want Rosalee to think I'm a coward."

"Yancy's a mean one."

"I said I'm going with you."

They both looked down as Carter jerked and died. The big man lay staring into space. Hank knelt and closed Carter's eyes. The women began to sob.

"Cover him up," Hank told them.

He and Gibney went into the kitchen and helped themselves to provisions. They took slickers and filled their canteens at the well. All the while, Gibney was figuring how he could make sure Hank didn't survive this trip.

"We'll have trouble trailing them," Gibney said as they mounted.

"I haven't mentioned it, but the Darringers are born trackers."

Leading the way on his black stallion, Hank leaned from the saddle as he rode, reading sign— bent grass, stones out of their socket, little things out of place, scratches on rocks. Sometimes, he was lucky enough to see the hoofprints of three horses. The third was trailing and heavily laden.

"He has a packhorse," Hank said.

The trail led into the hills, south toward the river. It appeared that Yancy planned to ford the stream and cut back into the foothills, maybe seeking refuge in the mountains.

It was also obvious they would not catch up with him before nightfall. That was eating at Hank. His face grew hot, and sweat drenched his body as he thought of Rosalee with that dangerous, ugly man.

"You see anything?" Gibney asked as they neared the river.

"We're on their trail, but they're gaining."

"My horse is getting worn out."

"Turn back."

"And let you be the hero?"

Hank just grunted and reined his horse on the riverbank. The raging waters, twenty feet wide, were shallow enough for a good horse to make it across. Cottonwoods lined the banks. There were signs where Yancy had fought his way over to the other side.

Hank led the way, his big stallion having no trouble with the rapids. Gibney's horse nearly fell more than once. At last they reached the other bank, where Hank took time to make an arrow of little rocks in case a posse came. He figured they'd be too late to do any good, but being late, they also would not be in the way or cause danger to Rosalee.

Hank noticed signs that indicated Rosalee had tried to ride away. Yancy had followed and somehow caught up her horse, turning her back.

Night was upon them as they headed southwest through the hills, away from the river, their backs to the town and the mines. Now it was too dark to see the trail. Clouds were covering the moon and most of the stars. They made camp in a hollow near a grove of aspens. A noisy stream trickled where the horses were tethered.

Sitting around the small, flickering fire, holding their hands out to its warmth, the two men studied each other. At one time, they could have been friends. Then they had shared a friendly rivalry over Rosalee. Now something else was between them, but Hank couldn't quite read it.

"That Yancy must be insane," Gibney said, sipping his coffee.

"Let's say it's true what he says about her being part Indian. Would you still want to marry her?"

"Of course I'd marry her. She needs someone to run her father's bank. And I'll give her respectability."

"Because you went to Harvard."

"And because I'm going to be someone important someday."

"Gibney, you are so full of hot air, I'm just going to sit around and wait until someone blows a hole in you."

The editor grinned. "You're just jealous. But I'll tell you what I'm going to do for you as a consolation prize. I think I should write a book about all that's happened since you hit town."

Hank merely grunted and sipped his coffee.

"You come riding in," the editor continued, "on some sort of vengeance trail because Harrington was your cousin. Next you kill the Smith boys. Then you go to arrest Tanner, thinking he's France, and you have to kill him. Some fellow keeps taking shots at you. Then Rickles accidentally kills Melanie Sloan and gets tried for murder. Quite a story."

"You haven't mentioned Yancy."

"Oh, yes, the bounty hunter, getting his posters one by one from Stumpy, who spends his time going through Smite's wastebasket."

"Stumpy get money from you?"

"Nice try," Gibney said with a smile. "I did humor him now and then with some money for the stories he'd bring. Nothing more."

"What about Rickles? Did you pay him?"

Gibney frowned. "You're trying my patience, Marshal. I haven't done anything wrong. I told you, I'm an educated man. I don't have to steal to make a living."

"You've never made a mistake?"

"Never."

Hank leaned back against his saddle, setting his cup aside. "You take first watch."

Gibney looked strained. "You mean he might backtrack?"

"He's no fool. Just watch yourself."

Gibney thought of Carter and old Tom, all cut up. A chill ran down his body. He watched Hank close his eyes and drop off to sleep.

For a moment, Gibney considered killing Hank here and now. He could use a knife and blame the bounty hunter. It would end his worries for good. But Gibney was no tracker. And Yancy still had Rosalee.

Gibney knew he needed Hank for now, but he was determined Hank would not survive. Somehow he would have to kill the marshal, if Yancy didn't do it for him.

Then he would comfort Rosalee, marry her, and take over all her father's holdings. He would be someone. Maybe he'd go into politics. What made it all so pleasant was that he really did love her. Every time she smiled at him, she made him feel as if he were king of the hill.

He stood up, rifle in hand, gazing into the darkness. He wasn't going to let Hank or anyone else ruin his chance to marry Rosalee and live in luxury. He was counting the days until he would no longer have that dirty ink on his hands and clothes.

After midnight, he awakened Hank.

"Hear anything?" Hank asked, sitting up.

Gibney shook his head as he sought out his blankets. Then he rolled up near the fire. Hank got to his feet and picked up a Winchester, moving out of the light.

He had not slept well. All he could think of was Rosalee, out there with Yancy.

While Hank worried and fretted, Rosalee was seated by a campfire in the far sweep of the hills. The camp was in a narrow ravine. The burning wood crackled and popped. She moved closer, warming her bound hands. She hurt from the beatings he had given her when she had tried to escape. Her ankles were swollen from the rawhide strands that bound them.

Yancy was standing nearby, listening to the cry of a nighthawk. He waited, but it wasn't repeated.

Then he knelt, and she drew back, eyes wide. His Spanish accent did not soften her fear as he spoke. "Do not worry. I will not touch you until it is time."

"What do you mean?" she whispered.

"When a man has to fight, he must think only of his enemy."

"My father will come after me. I don't want him hurt."

"I left no tracks."

"Please, you must let me go."

"No, I will never let you go, little one."

She stared at him, at his small black eyes and straggly black hair. Her fear was so intense, none of this seemed real. Her voice sounded far away. "Even if I don't want to stay?"

"You are Indian, like me."

Helpless, her body cold and stiff, she knew it was useless to argue with him. Maybe she should humor him, get him to relax so that when there was a chance to escape, he would be off guard. And it felt good to say the words she had been choking down for so long: "You're right. My mother was one-quarter Cheyenne. My grandmother died at Sand Creek. But I didn't know them."

Yancy was pleased with her words. "Now you speak the truth. You have hated living a lie."

"Yes, but my father told me I had to keep the secret. He said the town would shame me."

"But it won't be that way in Mexico."

She drew her blanket around her. His face had become kinder since she had stopped trying to run away. Earlier, he had beaten her with his fists until she realized she couldn't escape. She hurt all over from the pounding.

If she was to survive until help came, she would have to be submissive. It was important to keep him talking. Soon her father would come. Or Hank Darringer. Or Gibney. Someone would be following, she prayed.

As Yancy spoke again, she sat fascinated by his deep, cultured voice. "My mother was Spanish, but she was a schoolteacher and taught me English. My father was Comanche. When he took her, she fought. But one day she married him. For that, I will wait."

"Where is she now?"

"Both were murdered by outlaws."

"Is that why you turned bounty hunter?"

"It made it easier."

Seeing him as human, finding he had a soft side, she felt a little less terrified. She wanted to ask him why an educated man would continue to look the way he did, wild and fierce. His brutal way of life belied his education. He was two men, it seemed.

She stared into the leaping flames. She was afraid even to guess where old Tom and her father were. Yancy had saddled her mare, which had waited with his own buckskin and a packhorse out behind the mansion. The knife at her throat had kept Rosalee silent. By now her father had to be frantic.

"Give me your word not to run away," Yancy said, "and I'll untie your hands and feet."

"For tonight."

He accepted that and used his huge knife to cut the thongs. Relief came to her as the pain subsided. She rubbed her wrists and ankles. As she sat there working to restore their circulation, she knew he was still watching her.

"If we were in the Nations," he said softly, "many braves would be fighting over you. Your heart is all Cheyenne. I have seen the fire and spirit. You are too strong for that newspaperman. Now, the marshal, that would be different. He is a warrior, like me."

He stood up and moved out of the firelight. Rosalee, weary and aching, lay back in her blankets. She had given up the idea of escape for tonight. As it was, she was afraid she wouldn't be able to move at all in the morning. She was hurting more and more as the shock began to wear off. But at last exhaustion put her to sleep.

While Rosalee slept, Hank was pacing about his own campfire, furious, frustrated, and frantic. Morning seemed to come so slowly, he wanted to scream at the horizon. At first light, they broke camp, saddling and riding south once more.

Dark clouds were moving in from the west, embracing the snow peaks and shadowing the foothills. It was colder. The sun was casting a sallow glow that was gradually being swallowed by the moving clouds.

Hank knew that Yancy was a fearsome enemy. At any moment, the man could spring from behind serviceberry bushes, or out of the earth itself. The Comanche were fierce warriors, and Yancy was half Comanche. The man had no fear.

Soon, they came to the abandoned campsite. Hank dismounted to read the signs. The ashes had been covered only casually. Yancy was either confident or knew they were on his trail and was setting up an ambush.

Hank knew there had been several struggles. Rosalee had tried to run away at the river, and she had even tried to escape on foot. It was obvious she had been beaten. Pieces of rawhide thong made it clear she had been bound.

"What do you see?" Gibney asked anxiously.

"Signs of brutality."

Gibney shook his head, but he knew Hank was right. Men could act like animals. He had proved it was true of himself, in Dodge and again in Prospect with Rickles and Smite. He wondered if Hank had ever lost control. As they rode on, he turned to the lawman. "How'd you get started wearing a badge, anyhow?"

"Tried it and liked it. Then I ran into Harrington, my cousin. Worked with him. He made it all seem mighty important."

"So's the written word. But I'll be giving it up when I marry Rosalee. I'll be too busy running things for her. I've even been thinking of startin' a tollway up to the mines."

"You're a man with big ambitions, Gibney."

They rode in silence, trying to go on breathing easily. Something told them that they were closing in on their prey. Fear froze their hearts, because they knew that any moment, one or both of them might die.

Chapter Nine

*T*hat afternoon, Hank read the sign on a path up toward the snowcapped mountains. They reined up, and he pointed the way the bounty hunter was headed. The sky was dark and threatening. It felt damp already.

"There's still a lot of snow up there," Gibney said. "There could be more. Look at that sky."

Hank knew the editor was right. They were running out of time. If it rained or snowed, he could lose the trail. He continued to mark trees and lay rocks, not only to find their way back if necessary, but to guide a posse.

The trail became steep and hazardous as they moved through the foothills and upward, leading them through sliding rocks and wet, treacherous earth. Night came on them. The clouds hung low, damp, and threatening. They were forced to camp in a narrow canyon.

There was a brief rain shower during the night. Huddled during his watch, Gibney sat studying the sleeping lawman. He longed to kill him now. Yet he had to wait. It made him furious that he needed Hank for tracking.

He fantasized how it would be to rescue Rosalee and tell her that Hank was dead. The minute he knew they were hot on the trail and close, he would shoot Hank in the back of the head. Then he would find a way to ambush Yancy.

In the morning as they moved on, Gibney's bay was stumbling more and more from exhaustion. The black stallion took the grade in its stride, never short of breath, its great muscles working easily.

The weather became colder, wetter, the sky dark.

They passed a deserted cabin near a mine shaft. The door was hanging sideways, and there were no windowpanes. A stack of cut wood had been left in the lean-to. They moved onward, keeping the place in mind for the return trip.

They started another climb. The rugged uphill land was set with heavy brush.

Now the rain started. They pulled on their slickers.

Suddenly, the bay lost its footing on a steep rise. Gibney and the animal went crashing back down the grade, sliding more than a hundred feet back to a narrow flat. The horse rammed against a tree. Both horse and rider went down, then the animal sprang to its feet, a foreleg dangling.

Hank rode back down. The editor was frantic, sitting up and holding his painful right leg. Ignoring Gibney's fretting, Hank knelt to check the horse's foreleg. "Just a sprain. But you can't ride him."

Gibney pleaded that his leg was shattered, so Hank allowed him to ride the stallion. On foot, he led the bay downhill, back to the cabin.

Inside, he built a fire in the iron stove. He checked Gibney's leg and determined it was not broken. He left Gibney a rifle and provisions. Just in case, Hank also made him a crutch out of a forked limb, and he hauled in most of the wood, stacking it near the iron stove. He reset the door and replaced the wooden windowpanes.

"If I don't make it back," Hank said, "you should be able to get down the mountain. It's likely a posse will be here soon."

"Blast!" Gibney said, fretting because Hank would be rescuing Rosalee without him. Still, he felt he wouldn't look too bad to her. He had been hurt trying to save her.

Gibney decided he would wait a couple of days, then follow Hank's trail. The lawman would be leaving marks for the posse. Gibney would just follow the signs. Then he would try to get rid of Hank at the right moment.

Unaware of the danger, Hank left Gibney in comfort, but he knew he could move faster now. His stallion could make its own speed. He rode back up the grade in the drizzling rain, knowing that any minute he could be in Yancy's sights.

*   *   *

Watching from far above in the forest, the bounty hunter sat quiet in the saddle. Snow patches spread through the pines. Rain was sprinkling down with a new chill.

Rosalee was weary in the saddle, her black mare already showing signs of coming up lame. The packhorse was sturdier. Yancy's buckskin was of mountain stock and unshaken by the elevation or climb.

Yancy knew that Hank would be gaining, however. That black stallion was hindered by nothing. Once he killed Hank, he would take the animal for himself.

It would be easy to stash Rosalee somewhere and then set up an ambush, but Yancy wanted her to think of him as a warrior with honor.

So in midafternoon, when Hank rode into a wide clearing in the forest, he was startled to see his prey waiting for him patiently. Over by the trees, the helpless Rosalee was sitting in the saddle, her hands tied, the packhorse near her. She was wearing a slicker and Yancy's buckskin hat to protect her from the drizzling rain.

Yancy was sitting solidly on his horse, his gun in his holster. He looked all Comanche in his buckskins, his straggly black hair wet and gleaming. His square face wore a sinister expression as he narrowed his small black eyes.

Hank rode within twenty feet of Yancy before reining up. His rifle was in the scabbard. His Colt was in its holster. Knowing that the tension of the moment could explode if he was not careful, he slowly drew his leather coat away from his holster, then put both his hands on the pommel. "Yancy, you're under arrest."

"I'm afraid you'll have to use more than words."

"This isn't a game. Unbuckle your belt."

"No, Marshal. If you must shoot, go ahead. The lady will see that you're a coward."

Realizing he was being forced into a showdown, Hank sized up the situation. Even if he could take away Yancy's gun, Yancy's knife would be too deadly. The man was not afraid of being shot down, that was clear. Hank grimaced. Yancy was setting him up.

The bounty hunter carefully dismounted, leaving his buckskin tied to the ground. Yancy walked to one side as Hank dismounted. Then he stood facing Yancy, their eyes locked. It was drizzling and cold, a terrible place to die.

"I've seen you draw," Yancy said coolly. "I know I'm faster, Marshal."

"This isn't necessary. I don't want to kill you."

"I'm not worried, but let me tell you that Stumpy knows who killed Harrington."

"What do you mean?"

"Stumpy saw it happen. But I could never pay him enough to tell me who it was. The killer paid him more."

The news was important, but the moment held Hank's attention. His body was numb, and sweat trickled down his face and back. He knew that this moment, if he did not die, would be the closest he had ever come to death. It wasn't just that Yancy might be faster, but that Yancy was not afraid to die, and that made him a cold, violent machine.

Still, the man had a strange sense of honor, not wanting to risk dying without telling Hank about Stumpy.

"Either drop your gun or make your move," Hank said.

Yancy smiled, a sneer that made his square face ugly.

There was a long, silent moment as they waited. Then suddenly Yancy drew, firing and creasing Hank at his sore left shoulder. Hank had already drawn, his bullet slamming into Yancy's chest. They both staggered back from the impact as their shots echoed off the mountain.

Wild-eyed and frantic, Yancy tried to fire again.

Then the bounty hunter was dead on his feet. He fell face down in the mud, where he lay sprawled and lifeless.

Hank holstered his gun. He felt his bleeding shoulder, muttering to himself. Then he turned to see Rosalee riding forth. She dismounted and ran toward him.

Pausing a few feet from him, out of breath, she was anxious and afraid. Her blue eyes were wet with tears.

"Are you all right?" she asked.

He nodded. She stood poised, though still shaken by her ordeal. The sight of him riding into the glen had brought hope. Now she was really safe. Her courage could be set aside.

She ran into the shelter of his right arm and pressed against him, her face to his chest. He held her a long moment. His heart was pounding with relief. She was safe at last and seemingly unharmed.

"Thank you," she whispered, drawing back.

He untied her hands, then allowed her to open his coat and rip his shirt where the bullet had creased him. She used his bandanna to press the slight wound, which was near his previous injury. He liked her gentle touch.

"Gibney's down the mountain with a sore leg," he said. "There's shelter there."

"Did my father come with you?"

Hank swallowed, his gray eyes narrowed. He fought for the words to tell her. He could only shake his head.

"Is he all right?" she asked, suddenly fearful.

"He's dead. And Tom was bad hurt, but I figure he'll be all right."

"Dear God, be with him," she prayed aloud, then asked, "Was it Yancy?"

Hank nodded, hurting for her.

She fell into his embrace, her face pressed to his chest, her arms around him, hugging him as she wept. Sobs shook her body. He held her tight with his right arm.

"All this time," she sobbed, "all the while I was talking with Yancy, he knew he had killed my father. He said he had honor, but he didn't."

Hank looked down at her satiny black hair as he drew aside the buckskin hat. He ran his fingers through her hair, caressing her shoulder. Then she slowly drew back, looking up at him. Tears were trickling down her lovely face.

"Maybe he didn't want me ever to know," she said.

He nodded, wishing he knew words of comfort.

For a moment, she just stood there, gazing up at him. She was so beautiful. He hated to see the bruise on her right cheek.

Hank had to struggle to drag Yancy's body over by the trees. He found soft ground and dug the best grave he could with the small shovel he found on Yancy's packsaddle. Rosalee made a cross of twigs tied with Yancy's rawhide strings.

Hats in hand, they stood together in the drizzling rain, looking down at the crude grave.

"Lord, rest his soul," Hank said grimly. "I never knew a sadder man."

As they turned away, he found Rosalee staring at him.

"Why did you say that?" she asked.

"He was half white, but no white man would respect him. He was half Comanche, but too civilized to live among them. He was an ugly man, but he was intelligent. He had honor, letting me know about Stumpy in case he was killed and I wasn't. Yet I know he killed men in cold blood."

"Do you know he wanted to marry me in a mission?"

"That proves I was right."

"Hank, if I told you something, would you promise never to tell anyone?"

They reached her mare and the other animals. She turned, looking up at him in the rain, waiting. He nodded.

"My mother," she said, "was one-quarter Cheyenne."

He nodded, rain dripping from his hat. "I know."

"And how do you feel about it?"

"I like it fine."

A lovely smile crossed her lips as she gazed up at him. Hank helped her mount the mare. She sat gazing down at him as she spoke. "What do you think Nelson Gibney would say if I told him?"

"Why don't you find out?"

"You're wrong about him. He's a good man and my father's choice."

Hurt, Hank turned to his stallion. He took the reins of Yancy's horse and handed them to her. Then he took the lead rope of the packhorse and mounted his black.

Together, the other horses following on lead, they rode back down the mountain. Hank pulled his slicker in place and sat hunched in the saddle. Yancy's buckskin hat was back on Rosalee's head, shielding her from the rain. The slicker she wore was too large, but it was keeping her dry.

When they reached the cabin, it was almost dark.

They took the horses over to the lean-to. Only his stallion and her mare would fit inside with the bay. The others would have to stand by the nearby shed. She helped him unsaddle. He lowered the load of furs and provisions from the packhorse. Yancy had figured to hole up for a long time.

Rifle in hand, he led the way toward the cabin. The hills were silent. Light snow was falling. It was pretty, soft and glistening.

Rosalee caught up with him at the door. She put her hand on it as she looked up at him, her smile gentle. "Thank you for saving me."

Fighting the urge to draw her to him, Hank opened the door. She took her hat in hand as they entered.

Inside, Gibney was sitting on a handmade wooden chair, his sore leg resting on another chair. He was delighted to see them and made a big show of trying to stand. He sat back, letting them see how injured he was.

Rosalee went to him, kneeling and taking his hand. "Are you all right? Is it painful?"

"Yes. What about you?"

"He beat me a little, that's all. But Hank told me about my father, that Yancy had killed him and hurt Tom."

Gibney didn't like her sudden familiarity with Hank. He knew he still had to kill the lawman. Somehow he'd have to make it look like an accident.

Gibney put on a show of pain, and she comforted

him. Hank set about starting the evening meal, and she then took over. She told them some of the things Yancy had told her the night before in camp.

"Throw that hat away," Gibney said.

She leaned back in her chair, stared down at the floppy buckskin on the floor, and shook her head. "No, I want to keep it."

"He killed your father," Gibney reminded her.

"He was two men," she replied. "I want to remember that he gave me back my pride in myself. He made me realize I shouldn't be ashamed of who I am."

"Rosalee, don't," Gibney said, fearful of what she was going to say. "Nothing matters but you and me."

"So you know?" she asked.

"I don't know anything except that you were your father's daughter. That's enough."

"But I'm one-eighth Cheyenne."

"It doesn't matter," he said. "But you must never tell anyone else. They would shun you. And I couldn't marry you, don't you see?"

"What do you mean?" she asked.

"If everyone knew, how could I marry you? Why, my family would disown me. No, Rosalee, if you want to marry me and be respectable, you have to keep that secret."

She was staring at him as if she were seeing him for the first time. "You would be ashamed of me?"

"Not of you," Gibney said awkwardly. "I mean,

it's not your fault. Look, Rosalee, I love you, but you have to be practical."

"*Respectable* was the word you used," she said, rising from her chair. Her face was red, her head held high.

"Sit down and listen to me. We'll be married right away. You'll need a man to run things."

She turned her back to him and walked to warm her hands at the stove. They could hear the wind and sense the falling snow.

"It'll work, believe me." Gibney tried to convince her. "But you have to cooperate. Keep the secret, just as you did for your father. And you'll have to do something with your hair. People talk about it. It makes you look Indian. We can't have that, honey. You'll have to pin it up."

"I'll think about it," she said.

"Rosalee, I didn't mean to hurt you," Gibney pleaded. "I love you, but I didn't make the world the way it is."

Hank had been listening in silence. He wanted to step in and tell her he would marry her without question, but he realized she felt she had to marry Gibney because it had been her father's wish.

They settled down for the night, Rosalee refusing to talk any longer. She took the only bunk. The men spread bedding on the floor. All night the wind howled, whistling through the cracks. Often Hank would get up and put wood on the fire.

In the morning, as they ate a quiet breakfast, Gibney tried hard to make his peace with Rosalee.

Hank sat back and watched. Rosalee was cool to the editor, refusing to look at him. The buckskin hat was still on the floor, near where she had hung her slicker.

Gibney's mind was working. He hadn't yet figured how to kill Hank. On the way back, he could arrange an accident maybe, when Rosalee wasn't looking.

Suddenly, they heard shouting. Hank sprang to his feet, gun in hand, a reflex reaction.

"Look at him," Gibney said. "You're just a gun, Marshal."

Hank went to the window. "It's the posse," he announced.

He opened the door to the wind. The land around the cabin was sprinkled with snow that was already melting. He went outside, closing the door behind him. He pulled his hat down on his brow to keep the hazy sunlight out of his eyes.

Leading the twenty-man posse was McCoy. The big man leaned forward on his pommel, looking like a man with a purpose. They all wore slickers, which some were shedding.

"You find Miss Carter?" McCoy asked.

"Yes. She's inside."

"And Yancy?"

"He's dead."

"Gibney in there?"

"Yes, why?"

McCoy straightened. "We aim to hang 'im."

Hank was suddenly stiff. He looked from McCoy

to the others, mostly merchants, though there were a few miners, the mayor—and Stumpy.

"Why?" Hank asked McCoy.

"Seems like he was the one what got Smite and Rickles."

"And how do you know that?"

"Stumpy saw him comin' out the window."

"Where was Stumpy at the time?"

"Walkin' behind the barber's. He'd been to see the doc for a bellyache."

Hank looked at the worried Stumpy. "Why'd he wait so long to tell us?"

"He'd been drinking. Went back to the Silver Palace to finish a card game, but everyone was gone. He got drunk, told Sugar what he saw. What's more, he spouted off about a few other things."

"He tried to tell us afterward he'd made a mistake," a fat merchant said, "but we went into the alley and we looked some more. And we found this."

The fat man held up a man's white handkerchief, black with printer's ink and monogrammed with the editor's initials.

"Gibney deserves a fair hearing," Hank said.

"We'll give him one," McCoy told him. "We got the judge right here with us."

"Marshal, I've tried to talk sense to them," Winslow said, riding forward.

"We've had enough," McCoy declared. "We'll

get us a decent sheriff and clean up our own town. Right now, we're startin' with that fancy editor."

Hank looked over at the nervous Stumpy. He backed up to the door, uncertain just how to handle this. They were determined, and he couldn't hold them all off. He had to work on their sense of fair play. "Let Gibney speak his mind," he said.

"That's fair," someone called out.

Hank turned and opened the door, calling to Gibney. The editor came outside, curious and also forgetting his limp. Rosalee followed, standing near him. They were both flushed, as if they had been arguing inside the cabin.

The fat merchant held up the handkerchief. "Gibney, we found this in the alley by the jail. It's got printer's ink on it and your initials."

"So what?"

"And Stumpy saw you comin' out the window," McCoy added.

"Stumpy said that?"

The little man was sweating as the editor turned to glare at him. Stumpy was leaning back in the saddle on his mule, his little brown eyes wild. He pushed his hat back from his worried brow.

"It's a lie," Gibney said.

Stumpy nodded nervously. "Yeah, I was drunk." Sweat was running down his squashed-in face.

"You don't have enough," Hank told the posse. "You have a handkerchief that could have been

dropped anytime. You have a witness who was in-
toxicated."

"He's right," the judge agreed.

The posse was still hot to hang someone.

"All right then," McCoy said. "We'll just hang
Stumpy."

"Why?" Hank asked, surprised.

"Because when he was drunk, he bragged to
Sugar how he put the rope around Harrington's
neck."

For a moment Hank thought he would explode.
His heart began to pound like a hammer. He was
cold all over, stiff and angry. He looked at the little
man, who was sweating in the drizzling rain.

"It's a lie!" Stumpy cried.

"We're gonna hang you just the same," McCoy
told him.

"Who was there with you?" Hank demanded of
Stumpy.

"Cut the talk," a merchant snarled. "Let's string
'im up."

"Wait." Hank held up his hand. "Who helped
you hang Harrington?"

"It's all a lie!" Stumpy sputtered, frantic. "I
don't know nothin'!"

"All right," Hank said. "String him up."

The men moved in around Stumpy, thirsting for
his blood. One man had a rope, the noose already
prepared. They pounced on Stumpy and his nervous mount. Stumpy was yelling for them to get
away.

"Marshal!" the judge pleaded.

"No, let 'im hang," Hank said, turning his back.

He saw the stunned look on Rosalee's face as she stood helpless in the doorway. Gibney's hand was on her arm. The editor was white-faced, but he didn't move.

"Marshal!" Stumpy shouted. "Help me!"

They had already crowded around Stumpy and his mule, forcing him over to a cottonwood, throwing the rope over a great bare limb. Stumpy was squirming in the saddle.

Slowly, Hank walked toward them, certain that by now the little man was worried enough to talk. The men tied Stumpy's hands behind his back and put the noose around his neck.

Hank walked up and grabbed the reins of Stumpy's mule.

"If you don't want to hang," Hank said, "tell me who was with you when Harrington was killed."

"I didn't do it, Marshal!"

"But you were there," Hank prompted him. Hank held up his free hand, and the men paused. Their horses were restless, prancing around. He continued to hold Stumpy's mule. If he let go, the animal would be struck, and Stumpy would hang.

The little man knew it as he looked wildly at Hank. "I want a deal!" he cried.

"No deals!" someone shouted.

"Just a minute," the judge said, riding up. "We want the man who killed Harrington, not a little extortionist who doesn't have the guts to kill a snake."

"He's right," someone called out.

"All right," McCoy grunted. "What's the deal?"

"Prison," the judge said. "No hanging."

"Okay, all right," Stumpy said, sweating profusely.

"Who was with you?" Hank demanded.

"I was ridin' out by myself, down along the river. I saw a man shoot the marshal in the back. I got scared, but he wanted to make sure I didn't never tell no one, so he made me put the rope around Harrington's neck. He said he'd kill me if I didn't. But that's all I done."

Stumpy cleared his throat before continuing. "Harrington was still alive, but he was unconscious. I stood back and threw up when that feller dallied on his saddle and hanged 'im."

"Who was it?" Hank asked, his face hot in the rain.

"He said Harrington had been after him and Rickles, for what they done in Dodge."

"What was his name?" Hank demanded.

"Same feller I saw comin' out the jailhouse window after Rickles and Smite got it. Yeah, it was France. I mean Gibney. His middle name's France."

Everyone turned to the editor, but it was too late.

Gibney was standing behind Rosalee, his left hand around her throat. He was holding his six-gun in his right, pressing it to her side.

Winslow reached over and took the rope from Stumpy's neck. No one else moved. They watched, helpless. It was raining harder now. The wind was rising.

Hank started walking toward the editor.

"That's far enough," Gibney shouted.

Hank slowed his walk. Gibney's face was red with anger. "I'll kill her!" he shouted wildly.

"Let her go." Hank was still moving toward him.

"You come any closer, I'll pull the trigger."

"No, you won't. For, whatever else you are, you love this woman."

Fierce anger was rampant in Gibney. He stood transfixed as Hank slowly moved toward him.

"While you were outside," Gibney said, "she told me she wouldn't marry me, so what do I care?"

"Let her go," Hank said, pausing only ten feet away.

Gibney kept his grip on Rosalee. He had the drop on the lawman, and everyone thought Hank would die.

But Hank spoke calmly. "I'm taking you in, Gibney."

"I'm not planning to hang. Make your play."

"No need for that."

"Then let me ride out of here. I'll leave Rosalee somewhere safe."

"No chance."

The two men studied each other. Gibney seemed

dead set on either escape or an honorable death. With his gun already out, he figured he could fire before Hank could draw. He began to goad the lawman. "All right then. Yes, I killed Harrington. He took a long time to die."

Hank was hot with anger, but he moved closer.

Gibney was ready, hoping to unsettle him. "Sure, Marshal, he sniffed me out, all right. He got in my office drawer when I was away, saw an old nameplate with France on it. When I came back and saw what he'd found, I just headed down the river and left a trail. It was easy."

Gibney kept Rosalee against his side. She was pale, her eyes round and fearful. Her frantic fingers gripped his wrist as his hand was closing tight at her throat, making it difficult for her to breathe.

Eyes narrowed, Gibney turned his gun on Hank, sentencing him to death in cold blood.

In that instant, Rosalee suddenly jammed her elbow into Gibney's middle and kicked him in the shin with her boot. Grunting and startled, Gibney managed to keep his grip on her throat. She threw her weight against him. His angry grip nearly squeezed the life from her. He was momentarily distracted but again aimed at Hank and pulled the trigger.

Hank drew so fast, they both fired at the same time. A bullet thudded into Gibney's chest, dead center, as Rosalee broke free and fell against the cabin. Gibney staggered, doubled up in agony. His bullet singed Hank's collar.

Gibney dropped to his knees. He looked up, trying to speak. His mouth moved. No sound came out. Rain dribbled down his ashen face.

The judge had come to stand at Hank's side.

Rosalee was sitting up, shaken and nearly hysterical.

Slowly, white-faced, Gibney fell forward, crashing to the ground. The judge knelt to check for life, then rose, shaking his head. "He's dead. I wonder what he was trying to say."

"Maybe that he was an educated man," Hank said grimly.

Slowly Hank turned around to look at the posse. Stumpy was free, rubbing his neck and calling out to the lawman. "Hey, Marshal, maybe I'll get a reward for this."

Hank just shook his head as he turned to McCoy. "Take Stumpy back to town. Lock him up until we figure out what to do with him. And take Gibney with you. I'm sick of looking at him."

"That was one fast draw," McCoy said with awe. "Maybe you oughta stick around, Marshal. We could use you."

At length, the posse rode away, taking Gibney's body and Stumpy with them.

The judge shook his head as he spoke to Hank. "I don't know if Stumpy'll get prison, since he only acted in fear for his life. He didn't help with the actual hanging."

"Well, we'll find something," Hank said.

The judge mounted his horse and rode away to

follow the others. Trying to recover his composure, Hank stared after them.

His heart heavy in his chest, he thought of Stumpy's description of Harrington's death. At least his cousin had been unconscious when he was hanged. Still, it didn't ease the pain, especially when Gibney had added to the story.

Tears came to his eyes, tears for his idol, a man who had worn a badge with honor, a man others followed and respected. A man just like Hank wanted to be.

A hand touched his arm. He looked down at Rosalee. Her beautiful face was wet with tears, just like his.

She slid into his embrace, and he held her tight. The drizzling rain had turned to soft, floating snow.

They slowly turned and went back inside. It was a long while before he could talk. He sat at the table, his face in his hands. At length, he looked up to see her standing at his side.

She put her hand on his sore shoulder, and he winced. She drew out the bandanna, rinsed it in the bowl of water, and pressed it back inside his shirt on the wound. It had stopped bleeding long ago, but he liked her concern.

He turned in his chair, gazing up at her. "You turned Gibney down?"

There was a smile on her lovely face as she nodded. She leaned close, her long, soft hair caressing his arm and shoulder. He wondered if he dared ask for her hand. He couldn't read her thoughts. Darringers could read a trail in the rocks, but they never understood women.

Looking down at the circled star pinned to his vest, he remembered the oath he had taken. He would like to keep wearing it. He wondered what she thought about it.

Yet he felt he couldn't give her that kind of life. She would never know whether he was dead or alive. He would be gone for months at a time. There would be no one to protect her or her holdings. She'd be vulnerable.

Worse, he didn't want to be away from her, not for a day or an hour. Not if she would have him. He slid his arm around her waist as he spoke. "Prospect needs a sheriff. I think I'll apply for the job."

"It'll be dangerous."

"But necessary. I want a fit place for our children. Would you mind being married to a lawman?"

Her smile sparkled. Her blue eyes glistened. "No, but I won't pin up my hair."

"Good. It'll give me something to grab when I'm chasing you around the house."

Hank drew her down to his knee. She settled in his embrace and slid her hands up to his face and neck. Their kiss was warm with promise.